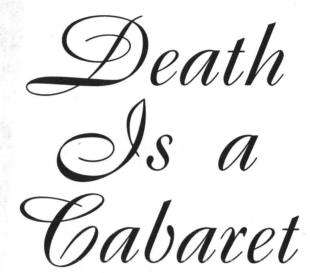

Death
Is a
Cabaret

Death Is a Cabaret

DEBORAH MORGAN

G.K. Hall & Co. • Chivers Press
Waterville, Maine USA   Bath, England

This Large Print edition is published by Thorndike Press, USA and by Chivers Press, England.

Published in 2002 in the U.S. by arrangement with the Berkley Publishing Group, a member of Penguin Putnam Inc.

Published in 2002 in the U.K. by arrangement with the author.

U.S. Softcover 0-7862-3929-8 (Paperback Series)
U.K. Hardcover 0-7540-4851-9 (Chivers Large Print)
U.K. Softcover 0-7540-4852-7 (Camden Large Print)

The text of this Large Print edition is unabridged.
Other aspects of the book may vary from the original edition.

Set in 16 pt. Plantin by Minnie B. Raven.

Printed in the United States on permanent paper.

British Library Cataloguing-in-Publication Data available

Library of Congress Cataloging-in-Publication Data

Morgan, Deborah (Deborah A.)
    Death is a cabaret / Deborah Morgan.
      p. cm.
    ISBN 0-7862-3929-8 (lg. print : sc : alk. paper)
      1. Antique dealers — Fiction.   2. Napoleon I, Emperor of the French, 1769–1821 — Art collections — Fiction.
    3. Large type books.   I. Title.
    PS3613.O668 D43 2002
      813'.6—dc21   2001051955

To my children,
Kevin and Kimberly,
my only perfect first drafts.
The legacy begins.

And to my precious grandson,
Dylan Ray, born at the same time as
the idea for this book.
May your own legacy outlast
the ink on these pages.

Acknowledgments

The author extends sincere appreciation to the following for their contributions:

Vicky Loyd, codirector of the Northfield Township Library, Whitmore Lake, Michigan, for everything from tracking down elusive books on antiques to offering chocolate and a printer when my computer crashed, along with my nerves.

Those wonderful and generous Michiganians on Mackinac Island: Dan and Amelia Musser, owners of the Grand Hotel; Bob Tagatz, historian, Grand Hotel; Anne St. Onge and Cindy Komblevitz of the Mackinac Island Public Library; and Police Lieutenant Pete Komblevitz.

Author Randall Platt and her husband Jonathan Platt, for Seattle expertise.

Editor Martha Bushko for her enthusiasm and knowledge, and agent Dominick Abel for bringing this opportunity my way.

Husband and comrade Loren D. Estleman: Thank you for many things, from two-way reading sessions in your study to French-pressed coffee at midnight.

Cabaret Sets

Cabaret set is a term used for eighteenth-century tea or coffee services, usually made of porcelain and including a teapot, coffee-pot, sugar bowl, creamer, cup and saucer, and tray. A service for one person was called a solitaire, a tête-à-tête was used for two. Breakfast services were sometimes termed *déjeuner.* Some were in fitted cases, which were at times as elaborate and costly as the sets themselves.

The specific cabaret set Jeff Talbot is pursuing in this novel is a result of the author's imagination. To her knowledge, no such set was commissioned by Napoleon. He did, however, commission many items from the Sevres Royal Porcelain Factory during his reign as French emperor, and at his hands a treasured set played an important role in history.

Following the victories of the Italian Campaign, while negotiating peace with envoys of Emperor Francis II of Austria, Napoleon flew into a rage and hurled a priceless cabaret set to the floor, shattering it. "This is what will happen to Austria!" he shouted. "Your empire is an old maidservant, accustomed to being raped by all and sundry." The Austrian diplomats, alarmed by this act of casual destruction, quickly agreed to his terms and signed the Treaty of Campoformio.

Chapter One

It was something you didn't often see on the expressway: a factory-condition '48 Chevy woodie, glossy black — it had, easily, twenty coats of paint — with gleaming wooden side panels from which came its nickname, and whitewalls like new ivory.

Traffic was on the cusp of the shift-change rush, and the woodie glided along, holding its own, its chrome winking at the passing one-coat wonders with their composite bumpers and similar shapes, like sausages on an assembly line.

Normally, Jeffrey Talbot would acknowledge the waves and smiles from others on the road who slowed down to admire the woodie's lupine beauty, but he was too preoccupied with the day's events.

The hour-long trip back to Seattle was just what he required. He rolled up his shirtsleeves, welcoming the late-afternoon sun that streamed through the windshield.

The heady scent of the car's leather mingled with the fragrant, aged musk of the antiques secured in back, creating an amalgam that permeated Jeff's senses and soothed him like a balm — a much-needed balm after today's run-in with Frank Hamilton.

It had started innocently enough. Both he and Hamilton had shown up at a home in rural Maple Valley where an estate sale was advertised to begin the next day.

The two men were antiques pickers, those largely behind-the-scenes individuals who hunted down items craved by an increasing onslaught of consumers interested in history or heritage or investment or, simply, a new way of decorating. Pickers looked for bargains, then turned a profit by reselling their found treasures to dealers, or private parties with specific tastes.

It was the pickers' grass-roots approach — search the classifieds for promising sales (estate, garage, moving) — then drop by early and try to cut a deal. This practice was called *high-grading.*

The two pickers had crossed paths several times, and Jeff had learned Hamilton's strategies, his habits, his tells, as though he were an opponent in a poker game. This trait of Jeff's was a holdover from his years with the FBI. Sometimes, Jeff suspected that his training with the Bureau was being put to better use now that he was working fulltime in the cutthroat world of antiques. He could predict Frank Hamilton's approach to buying antiques, probably before Hamilton himself knew it.

Hamilton's boyish charm had a sexual quality that Jeff suspected was his most valuable asset. This was obvious because he usually targeted women — and he usually succeeded.

Frank Hamilton displayed a different personality for each of three age groups:

The young ones, eyes sparkling in response to his flirting, said they had better things to do with their Saturday nights than spend them polishing Grandma's silver. Hamilton easily plucked a young thing of her sterling legacy, and she gave it up willingly.

With middle-aged women, he portrayed a college kid, far from home and missing Mommy. Most guys don't give their mothers a second thought once they're out from under the matriarchal thumb. But Mom doesn't know that. So, pretty young Frank cashes in. She gives him milk and cookies. She sews on loose buttons. She sends him home with leftovers — and an antique pedestal table. He's trying to make a little money for schoolbooks and, besides, what is she going to do with that gaudy old piece of furniture when he can get it out of her way and give her a little cash to boot?

Hamilton would later resell the table — with its *pietra dura* inlay, trinity of carved dragons at the feet, and maker's signature with his Florence address included, no less — for enough to keep him in Italian loafers till someone outlasted Mussolini.

With the elderly, Hamilton was an odd combination of politeness and urgency. He got them to warm up to him, then he turned up the heat: This deal won't be around tomorrow! You'd better act fast! You're going to lose out!

Hamilton had been trying this last method on an old lady when Jeff showed up today.

Only it appeared that he'd forgotten to add the charm.

The large, two-story clapboard house sat off by itself twelve miles from Interstate 90, southeast of Seattle. Jeff had eased the woodie down the long driveway, gravel crunching beneath the tires. He'd recognized Hamilton's old Ford pickup near the house.

Hamilton, in his customary uniform of T-shirt, jeans, oversized sport coat, and loafers without socks, was having a heated discussion with a squat, white-haired woman in faded overalls and a red checkered blouse.

Jeff parked a couple of car lengths back from the pickup and sat there, watching. Suddenly Hamilton popped his forehead with the heel of his left hand. It wasn't the first time Jeff had seen the young picker do this, and he knew what it meant: Hamilton was dangerously close to losing it. Jeff stepped out of the woodie and approached the two slowly. He wanted to be close enough to help the elderly woman if Frank didn't back down, but he also wanted to be far enough away so that she wouldn't feel he was threatening her as well.

Just then, she produced a cell phone from her left pocket and, without breaking eye contact with Hamilton, punched the keypad with her left thumb. Jeff barely heard the three soft beeps over Hamilton's voice, but Frank seemed to have heard them loud and clear, because his mouth clamped shut.

The woman eyed the young picker fiercely. "You get the hell out of here now, or I'll hit Send."

Hamilton didn't budge.

"I didn't get this old by bluffing. Now, *git!*" She lunged toward the young man. He stepped back. Jeff figured Frank wasn't afraid, merely surprised by the old woman's sudden movement.

Nonetheless, it had the desired effect. Hamilton mumbled something about her missing out, then stomped toward his pickup. He jumped when he saw Jeff, stopped briefly to glare at him before climbing into the cab. After grinding the starter to its core, Hamilton got the motor to turn. He threw the truck in gear and took off. It lurched over the lawn, shaved past the woodie, and managed a skidding left turn at the end of the driveway.

Jeff looked at the woman and chuckled. "I was about to offer my services, but it appears you don't need them."

"What? Oh, this." She held up the phone. "I'd already be dead and buried if I thought this would bring the local yokels out here in time to help me."

She eased her other hand from the right pocket of the overalls. It held a .38 caliber snub-nose.

Jeff grinned.

The old lady grinned. "My peripheral vision is still intact. You were cool as iced tea back there, not skittish like that kid. Are you a cop?"

"FBI. Used to be, anyway. I switched to antiques because I wasn't seeing enough action."

The woman chuckled, then motioned for Jeff to follow her.

Later, approaching the interstate on-ramp with a carload of antiques from the old woman's garage, he'd seen Frank Hamilton's pickup on the shoulder of the road.

He almost went on past. Then he cursed, pulled in behind the Ford, and rolled down the window. Hamilton, who had been leaning against the truck's bed, walked toward him.

"Did she quit you?" Jeff asked, indicating the pickup.

"Nope," Hamilton muttered as he walked past the driver's window. "Just wanted to see if you'd gotten past the old lady's crappy attitude."

Jeff considered telling Frank who had the attitude, but he let it slide. He got out of the car.

Hamilton peered through the back glass. "What the hell? How . . . ?"

"Just good business, Frank. You wouldn't recognize it."

"I make out fine."

Jeff opened the hatch — in his opinion, those SUV owners had nothing on his station wagon — and repositioned a wooden box packed with bubble-wrapped statuary that was crowding a pristine wicker perambulator. It was rare to find one of these old baby carriages that hadn't either been painted to within an inch of its life, damaged from storage in damp basements and outbuildings with leaky roofs, or abused beyond repair while being used as a toy by the very children who had once lain swaddled in its shelter. He straightened, looked at Hamilton. "What happened to you back there?"

"I was there first, man. You know the rules."

"Rules?" Jeff's rule book contained two: Do Unto Others (the original one, not the smart-mouthed spin-offs), and The Customer Is Always Right.

"Yeah, rules." Hamilton smirked. "You've

been at this long enough to know the damn rules."

Jeff's expression didn't change. At thirty-seven, his hair hadn't started turning gray, and it hadn't started turning loose, either. He wouldn't go back to being Hamilton's age, even if the deal included *Whistler's Mother*.

"You were coming on too strong, Frank. She had to order you off her property, for God's sake. Don't you know how to take a hint from a woman?"

"I've never had any complaints." Hamilton swaggered up to the woodie, and it was as if he'd seen the perambulator for the first time. He reached into the back of the car and gently stroked the soft lining. Suddenly, he turned and hurried toward his pickup.

While a perplexed Jeff contemplated the contradictions in the man — harsh bravado, then gentle reflection, then abrupt flight — Hamilton turned again. The rebel mask was back in place. "You think people don't talk about your secrets in that fancy house on the hill, old man?" He spat the words out bitterly, leaning on *old man,* but his voice had a nervous edge to it.

Jeff smiled. He'd heard the rumors about his home life. They ranged from harmless speculation (he had a harem of women at his bidding), to downright sinister (he had an old aunt who'd gone berserk and was kept locked in a room on the third floor). There

16

were more false stories told about his personal life than there were fakes in the antique world.

Before Jeff could respond, Hamilton had said, "Don't ever move in on my game again. Understand?" He had vaulted into the pickup's cab and headed up the ramp to I-90.

Now, trying to sort through this bizarre chain of events, Jeff almost missed his exit. He quickly checked the rearview mirror, then swerved and caught the inside of the vee.

Episodes like the one with Hamilton made Jeff wonder if he should go back into law enforcement. Just as quickly, though, he recalled why he'd left in the first place.

He'd grown weary of tracking missing art and antiques — operative word, *missing*. He'd rarely had any actual contact with antiques.

Oh, occasionally, he'd go undercover to make a buy. The FBI doesn't have an art theft unit as such, but the machine operates efficiently. The Bureau's corner-office crowd learned of Jeff's genuine love for antiques and figured that gave him an edge over other field agents. He was first-call when they needed a buyer. The problem was, it didn't happen that often. Most things went missing and stayed missing. Some things stayed underground forever.

He saw photos from museum files and artists' records whose works had been stolen from galleries. He saw curators' offices and fronts for illegitimate fencing operations. He spoke with somber-faced security guards who didn't know if they'd be looking for employment by the end-of-the-week whistle, and thugs who'd give their right ears before they'd give you a lead on a missing Van Gogh.

As a buyer, he saw the high-pressure salesmen: sleazes who wouldn't guarantee a provenance, scumbags who danced around issues of origin and skirted direct questions about an object's owner.

The go-betweens, that's who he'd dealt with. Every damn one of them. Go-betweens.

He'd gotten out fast — stunning his fellow field agents, his squad leader, everybody. He wanted to be on a higher road. He wanted to rescue antiques from the basements, storage buildings, and yard sales where people either let them gradually go to ruin or sold them for a few bucks to others who slapped a coat of paint on them with no regard to possible value.

Jeff looked upon his current profession as more of a calling. He was a champion of sorts, a savior of lost souls, a redeemer of things that couldn't redeem themselves.

He thought about Hamilton, wondered how the young picker would behave the next time they ran into each other. And they *would* run into each other. No place was large enough to avoid the likes of Hamilton when you were in the antique business. Not even Se-attle.

Especially Seattle.

The Emerald City loved its antiques, even if it didn't have a clue about how those antiques arrived in its quaint shops and antique malls. No matter. Jeff's veins were filled with the oil that fueled railroad lanterns, the linseed that preserved antique furniture, the inks of ancient documents, the pigments of masterpiece paintings. Antiques weren't merely in his blood; they'd replaced it a long time ago.

Jeff pulled into the parking lot of his favorite antique mall and consciously gave up trying to understand Frank Hamilton's motives. *Maybe he'll learn with age,* Jeff thought as he stepped out of the car and put on his Harris tweed. *If someone doesn't kill him first.*

Chapter Two

Blanche Appleby always got what she wanted.

Well, nearly always. As owner of Seattle's largest and most successful antique shop, All Things Old — "including me," she often said — Blanche could afford anything she desired. This kept Jeff — and no telling how many other pickers — busy flushing out bargains, then reselling them to Blanche in order to keep her store's inventory (and his own bank account) healthy.

Jeff always brought his finds to Blanche first. His reasons were purely mercenary: Blanche paid better than anyone else in the business.

She'd renovated an old warehouse down by the waterfront, customizing it into a three-story antique mecca. With the large parking lot, it took up a city block. The walls of the ground floor's formidable main room stretched upward twenty-eight feet, and a massive oak staircase led to a gallery that bisected the room's height. The Widow's Walk, as Blanche had named the gallery, was edged all around with an elaborately scrolled wrought-iron railing. It showcased a fortune in antique porcelains produced by European factories such as Sevres, Meissen, Chantilly, Minton, and Vincennes.

The rest of the main floor was segmented into several large rooms, which housed everything from toys to swords, from cut glass to gas pumps, from furniture to books.

The basement was split in half. On one side was TLC (Tender Loving Care), for the do-it-yourselfers, with barrister bookcases in want of glass and chairs whose seats needed recaning. On the other side was George's, named for Blanche's late husband. George's was jam-packed with antique tools, weathervanes, fishing gear, sports and railroad memorabilia, and architectural hardware. Although she showed no propensity toward discrimination of the sexes, Blanche Appleby assigned railroad china to George's as well in order to entice those females who might not normally frequent such places.

Dominating the third floor was The Cabbage Rose, a tea room that offered a large luncheon menu including three varieties of quiche, several homemade desserts and, in answer to Seattle's major obsession, more blends of coffee than any other establishment in the city.

When questioned about her penchant for naming the sections of her establishment, Blanche declared that she would call the bathrooms Fred and Ethel if she took a mind to. George and Blanche never had children.

Jeff rolled the ornate perambulator into the lobby. Around him, the wooden floors creaked and sighed under the steady current of people who had sought out Blanche Appleby's coastal paragon. They, like so many others, had greeted the new millennium with a firm reach backward. When the population in general had looked in their garages on January first and found that hovercrafts hadn't replaced their Oldsmobiles, they'd embraced the past as surely as they had anticipated the present.

He strolled past the large L-shaped counter where customers were stacked six deep, waiting to make their purchases as closing time neared. As he walked, his eyes darted quickly over the antiques, and he tried to identify what had been added and what had sold since his last visit. Not only was he always searching for items to add to his own collections, but also he liked to know what had been brought in by other pickers.

Blanche's office was near the end of a long hallway. The door was open.

She was seated behind an immense French provincial desk, writing furiously in a ledger. Her fiery personality and bright red hair made her seem larger than she was. In fact she was only four feet eleven. Under the desk, her slippered feet were planted squarely upon a tapestry-covered footstool. She admitted to being seventy, but she neither looked it nor acted it.

He rapped the doorjamb lightly.

She looked up. "Jeffrey!" She closed the ledger with a thud. "What does my favorite treasure hunter have for me today?"

"Favorite? You mean I'm not your only picker?" Jeff tried for a hurt look, but he couldn't wipe the grin from his face.

"I'll give you this. You're the only picker I know who doesn't *look* like a picker."

"I'll take that as a compliment." Jeff retrieved the pram from the hallway and wheeled it into the office.

Blanche shot out of her chair. "I haven't seen one of these in years!"

"I know you're not old enough to have ridden in one like this."

She wasn't listening. "It's more like a coach or a surrey than a pram. Watch this." She worked some pulleys, and fringed side panels rolled up to give full view of the interior. Blanche caressed the tufted upholstery, scrutinized the weave of the wicker, tilted it to check underneath. She located a small brass identification plate. "Heywood-Wakefield. That puts it just before the turn of the twentieth century — the two companies were competitors before that. It's an extraordinary piece, Jeffrey. Absolutely top of the line." She turned to the bookcases directly behind her desk. From this reference library containing hundreds of volumes, she quickly chose a few books on wicker furniture, then sat at her desk and began leafing through pages.

While Blanche searched, Jeff thought about the food chain. So many factors came into play when dealing with antiques: the fickle public, regional demands, quality, condition. Today, Jeff had paid a hundred dollars for the carriage, and he could expect to get triple that from Blanche. She, in turn, would sell it for at least triple what she paid him, and the treasure would likely be snatched up and in its new home before the weekend was out.

Jeff took a slim brown leather-bound notebook from the breast pocket of his jacket. "There's more, Blanche. You're going to love me."

"More than I do now? Impossible." She motioned toward the chair opposite. "Have tea with me before you start traipsing back and forth. It's been a day."

He couldn't disagree with her about that. He sat.

She flipped the intercom switch. "Trudy, would you have the kitchen add another setting to my tea tray? Jeffrey Talbot is going to join me."

"Yes, Mrs. Appleby."

Blanche located the carriage in a book that covered fifty years of wicker furniture. Jeff recognized the volume. He had the same one in his home library.

"I thought it would be in this one." She looked up expectantly. "So, what else do you have for me?" She clapped her hands together twice, as if doing so would make all of it appear before her eyes.

Ceremoniously, he read to her from the list he'd compiled that afternoon. "There's a Tiffany lamp, turn of the century, I think; tons of old silver; a box of stuff for George's; and — you're not going to believe this — a *roomful* of Napoleonic items: Dresden statuary, books —"

"My cabaret set?" She bolted from her seat.

He stared at her for a moment before he realized what he'd done. A sinking feeling overtook him. How could he have been so careless? No excuse came to him, and all he could figure was that the run-in with Hamilton had thrown him off his game more than he'd thought.

"Blanche, I'm sorry. No."

She lowered herself back into the chair. She flipped the intercom switch again and asked Trudy what was taking so long with the tea. There was no response. She stood and paced the room.

Trudy's voice came over the store's loudspeaker, announcing that All Things Old would close in fifteen minutes and customers should make their way to the main counter with their purchases.

Blanche returned to her desk. After a few moments, she sat and gave Jeff a slight smile. "It's my obsession, not yours. You're just doing your job. And, Lord knows, I've exhausted enough leads over the years, searching for that tea set. I should be accustomed to disappointment."

She gazed for a while at the small lacquered box that she kept on the corner of the desk, then opened it and removed from it two old photographs.

Jeff knew what they were. One was of Blanche's mother, the other of the cabaret set Blanche had been searching for since she was a young woman. Jeff carried his own copy of the tea set's photo in his wallet, along with a photocopy of the set's letter of provenance.

"She died fifty-seven years ago today."

"I'm so sorry, Blanche."

A faint clatter could be heard from down the hall. Blanche propped the photos against the lacquer box as a small-framed girl in a blue calico dress shuffled in with a large silver tea service expertly balanced on her left shoulder. She bent her knees and slid the tray onto the credenza behind Blanche.

"Trudy, honey, I didn't mean for *you* to do this."

"I don't mind." Trudy poured the steaming

liquid. "The Cabbage Rose is shorthanded today."

The two women were complete opposites, and Jeff was still surprised at how well they seemed to get along. Trudy Blessing, Blanche's personal secretary, was a quiet and unassuming young woman of indeterminable height. Jeff had never seen the girl stand up straight. She seemed perpetually stooped, as if pulling in to herself. Jeff couldn't be sure whether this was out of some odd attempt at self-protection or whether it was simply a result of extreme shyness. She wore her mousy brown hair straight, with blunt bangs like one might find on a six-year-old. Her pale skin, unadorned by cosmetics, appeared even paler behind dark-rimmed glasses that looked like two saucers on her face.

In defense of her hiring choice, the older woman had said, "Put *two* spitfires under the same roof and somebody's going to get burned."

No chance of that here.

Trudy served the pair, then quietly left the room.

"When are you leaving for Michigan?" Blanche asked.

Jeff said, "I fly out tomorrow morning."

"They say the island will be stunning this year. The leaves are already turning, thanks to the heavy rains and early cold snaps."

"Then I should feel right at home, shouldn't I?"

Blanche chuckled without comment. One of many common bonds the two had was their love for Seattle's rainy climate.

They drank in silence, neither of them touching the plates of sandwiches and scones that Trudy had placed on the table.

Jeff studied the woman who sat across from him, saw the tiredness in her face. The brief visit to her past had aged her, and her efforts to be sociable couldn't hide it.

After she'd finished her tea, she carefully placed the old photographs back in the box. "It's not so much that I miss her, although there's that, too, of course. But I miss the *memories*, the things we shared during our brief time together. That tea set was the only thing she had to give me, and I'll never forgive the man who sold it out of my hands."

Jeff drank his tea and said nothing. He didn't dare share the rumor with her. If it turned out to be false, she'd be devastated. And she'd already been hurt enough. But he had heard that the cabaret set — Blanche's cabaret set — would be a last-minute addition to a special auction at the Annual Antiques Festival on Michigan's Mackinac Island.

When Blanche had first told him of the set, she'd also told him that she trusted him to be fair regarding the price if he ever acquired it. He trusted her, as well. He could purchase the set with the assurance of re-couping his money. He wasn't concerned with making a hefty profit on this one — just enough to cover his expenses.

The important thing was to get Blanche's cabaret set back for her. And he was going to do that, no matter what.

Chapter Three

Napoleon loved Josephine.

Napoleon loved Josephine fiercely, he loved her passionately. He drew strength from that love for the battles that would bring him power and wealth. Because of that love, he forgave transgressions that no ordinary man would tolerate.

It was a love from which he would never recover.

As his fortune grew, Napoleon gave his beloved bride many elaborate gifts. And the gift many believed she treasured most was a French cabaret set, commissioned from the Royal Porcelain Factory of Sevres.

Providing a theme throughout the set's design were Josephine's beloved swans. The curvature of their slender necks formed the golden handles on each piece of claret porcelain. The scenes painted upon the pearl-white cartouches that graced the bodies of the pieces featured swans as well, gliding upon flower-strewn waters.

The elaborate set took years to complete, the painstakingly wrought pieces arriving one by one at Malmaison via courier from the factory: serving tray, teapot, sugar bowl, creamer, a cup and saucer set for the empress.

A magnificent fitted case of black Moroccan leather gilded with gold and lined with ivory silk from Lyons was designed to house the porcelain.

The gift would have appeared complete by most standards, for a cabaret set typically contained only one cup and saucer. But Napoleon had commissioned a second cup and saucer set, in order that he might join Josephine in her private chambers for tea.

During those many years that she'd awaited the arrival of each porcelain piece, Napoleon had waited for an heir to his throne.

But the empress could not give him one.

And while the courier traveled toward Malmaison with the final pieces, a distraught Napoleon was reluctantly divorcing his Josephine.

The heartbroken empress couldn't bear to look at the cabaret set and gave it to her most loyal lady-in-waiting, a young woman named Isabelle Fougères.

Mme. Fougères would later pass the royal treasure into the hands of her daughter upon the young woman's betrothal. This established a tradition that was honored for generations.

That tradition stopped with a cruel blow, delivered to a descendant Isabelle Fougères would never know: a granddaughter's granddaughter named Blanche.

While Blanche was growing up, she and her mother often used the imperial cabaret set for afternoon tea. Before Blanche's father returned from work, and while her little sister was napping, Blanche would ceremoniously place scones in a woven basket lined with a frayed yet crisply starched linen cloth, take clotted cream and jellies from the aged but serviceable ice box in their tiny kitchen, and deposit it all on a makeshift butler's tray to be taken to the living room. Blanche's mother would brew peppermint tea, then carefully transfer it to the cabaret set, along with plenty of sugar and milk.

As mother and daughter shared afternoon tea, they chose an imaginary guest, usually Queen Victoria or the generous ancestor Fougères or the Empress Josephine. It was during these times that Blanche learned from her mother of her French heritage and of Napoleon and Josephine's great love affair.

The daily tea parties represented an oasis of calm for Blanche, before her father returned from work and the war between her parents resumed.

When her mother died suddenly, just after Blanche's thirteenth birthday, the girl withdrew from everyone and everything. It was only when she planned to marry, several years later, that she believed she could bear the thought of looking at the tea set. Blanche remembered her mother's promise that the cabaret set would become hers when she wed. When she couldn't find it, she learned that her father had sold the set out of the family. He would offer neither compassion nor explanation to the grieving young woman.

After her father's death many years later, Blanche discovered in the family's things the letter of provenance written by the Empress Josephine, confirming the set's imperial ownership. Along with the letter was an early twentieth-century photograph of the cabaret set, faded but easily recognizable to the girl who had cherished it.

This discovery had instilled new hope in Blanche Appleby, and she had been searching for her legacy ever since.

Although Jeff had heard Blanche's story of the cabaret set many times, he never grew tired of it. But as he started the ascent through his neighborhood, he put the set out of his mind. He reminded himself that he'd be spending the weekend thinking about it. Inquiring after it. Pursuing it. That would have to be enough for now.

Jeff eased the woodie into his driveway and pulled inside the small carriage house he used for a garage. He grabbed a package from the back seat and headed toward the house.

Dusk was descending quickly. He thought about tomorrow's trip and how much he looked forward to visiting Mackinac Island for the first time. He slowed down, giving himself a moment both to savor his excitement and to contain it. He hated to think that his enthusiasm might be misinterpreted by Sheila. She always assured him that she didn't mind staying home, but a part of him realized that he'd never fully adjust to always traveling alone.

The aroma of dinner met him as he climbed the seven steep steps to the back door.

The home, built of red brick that had darkened over the last century, was one of the original Queen Anne mansions built in a neighborhood named for that particular architectural style. Jeff was devoted to maintaining the home's original integrity. It was built by his ancestors and had been occupied by no one other than Talbot family members from the beginning — a desirable state for historical residences. He saw to it that the trim colors were never altered from what had been used when the mansion was built in 1890. The many shades of ivory, maroon, goldenrod, and olive were matched to original paint chips kept in the household files, a task made much easier in recent years with computerized matching. Jeff's Aunt Primrose Talbot (Auntie Pim) had begun teaching him these things about the house before he'd even received his first box of crayons.

In the kitchen, Sheila Talbot stood in front of the largest reproduction range made by the Elmira Stove Works (she called it her El Dorado, since she no longer drove), stirring the contents of a stockpot on the back burner.

Stretching the length of the immense room was an oak refectory table, its center stacked with Yellow Ware bowls and salt-glazed crockery. On the end of the table nearest the range was an assortment of fresh vegetables and herbs, waiting for the magic touch of the chef in residence. At the far end was her mail. Unlike Jeff's, which would be in the wall pocket in his study, this contained more boxes than envelopes. The trend would continue as Sheila increased her Internet shopping. It was a trend he not only welcomed but encouraged.

Sheila had the enviable ability to eat anything she desired without ever gaining an ounce, a good trait for someone who loved to cook. Her young, smooth skin and strong-boned features required no cosmetic camouflage. Either of these attributes might have caused jealousy among the female ranks and been reason enough for Sheila's lack of women friends. Neither was, however. She gave all she could to friendship; for most, it simply wasn't enough.

She wore a white chef's apron over khaki slacks and a crisp white shirt. Her long, straight, honey-colored hair was secured at the nape of her neck with a plain gold clasp.

Jeff believed his wife couldn't be any more beautiful. At times he was astounded that she'd ever given him more than a passing glance.

She looked at her husband like a teacher waiting for an answer to an oral quiz.

"Coq au vin," he announced, "with a signature Sheila touch . . . your home-canned basil tomatoes?"

Her brows arched. "You're learning." She replaced the pot's lid, then gave her husband a quick kiss and started to work on the vegetables.

Jeff gave a mental sigh of relief. It had been an educated guess. With all the vegetables in the chicken and wine stew, he wouldn't have known if she had, indeed, strayed from the recipe for the French staple.

A clatter came from the dining room.

Jeff wheeled. "What the hell?"

"Greer's redecorating his rooms, remember?" Sheila said. "He's been concerned that he won't finish before you get back, so I told him to go ahead and start putting things in the dining room. I assured him we wouldn't mind breaking Victorian protocol by having dinner in the breakfast room this one time."

Jeff chuckled. Although he and Sheila always ate in the dining room, it had nothing to do with the strict manners of the Victorians. Before Sheila moved in, Jeff ate in the living room on a TV tray. He played along with his wife's joke. "We can skip the dining room, as long as the ghosts of my ancestors don't rattle the chandeliers all night. I've got an early flight tomorrow."

"You're not the one who has to worry. They only rattle things while you're away."

"You love it." Jeff planted a kiss on her neck, then started toward the dining room.

"Don't take too long," she called after him. "I have a gift for your trip."

Jeff slid open the pocket doors. The Chippendale mahogany table had been fully extended and was draped with movers' quilts in order to protect its antique finish against scratches. In its center were two prints, double-matted in cream over black and in gilded antique frames that gave off a warm, burnished glow.

Greer darted in like a hummingbird, hovered momentarily before placing a stack of books on the table's matching buffet, then greeted his employer before darting back toward his own suite of rooms. He'd removed his customary uniform of black suit coat and tie, and his white shirt cuffs were rolled to his elbows.

The Talbots' butler was a slender young man, gay, with shingle-cut black hair, angular features, and the face of someone who'd begun shaving only last week. He had served the couple with loyalty and devotion since completing butler school six years before. Much about the traditional school of butling he'd learned from his grandfather and grandmother, who were butler and maid to a prominent European couple who had made their home in the States during the late sixties.

He had finished his training at an institution with an eye to the future — one that taught a new-school approach that would accommodate the wants and needs of households in the twenty-first century.

Greer was perfect for the unusual requirements of the Talbots.

Stacks of videos filled the table's matching sideboard, and Jeff didn't have to check the jackets to know which films they were. Greer owned a copy of every movie ever made that included a butler: *Arthur*, *My Man Godfrey* (both the '36 and the '57 versions), *How to Murder Your Wife*, *His Butler's Sister*, *Remains of the Day* — the list went on and on.

Jeff set his shopping bag on a side chair and turned his attention back to the art. The artist's name was Jack Vettriano. Jeff raised one of the frames slightly, shifting the glare away from the brass plate. "Interesting title," he said when Greer returned with another stack of books. "*Elegy for a Dead Admiral.*"

"The butler first drew me to it, of course," Greer said. "But it tells a story, too, when you combine its title with the ocean looming in the background." Greer lifted the second print. "This one is my favorite. It tells with one image what the proper attitude of a butler should be."

Jeff took a closer look at the second painting. The plate identified it as *The Singing Butler,* and in it a butler and a maid were holding umbrellas for a couple in evening dress dancing on the beach.

Greer snapped a cloth from his pocket and polished a spot on the glass. "The two paintings are very similar, yet completely different. Romance and death."

"Maybe not so different. The one about death has quite a romantic quality to it." Jeff admired the deep golds, blacks, and rich reds that dominated both prints. "I'd like to see if this artist Vettriano has something that might work in my study. His Art Deco style appeals to me."

"Yes, sir. I'll check the web and print out some samples."

Jeff couldn't help but smile as he left the dining room. If it weren't for Greer and Sheila, he'd think a web was simply a spider's way to catch breakfast.

Chapter Four

Sheila was removing a pear tart from the oven when Jeff returned.

"Perfect timing." She placed the fluted pan on a cooling rack and took him by the hand.

She led him into the drawing room and motioned him toward the settee while she went to the game table.

Beaming, she handed him a handsomely wrapped package.

"Where'd you go for this one?" Jeff removed the ribbon.

"TravelSmith. You should check out their site sometime."

"I'll leave the high-tech world in your capable hands. Is TravelSmith the latest, greatest destination on your Favorites list?" He said the company's name quickly, but couldn't pull off the single-word effect as she had.

"You think you have me figured out, do you?" She sat beside him.

"Let's see. Epicurious for recipes, Williams Sonoma for gourmet gadgets, eBay for antiques, Drugstore for your lotions and potions. Oh, I'm forgetting the dot com dot com dot —"

"Just open your present." Her eyes narrowed, but she was still smiling.

He pulled the vest from the box and examined it. He was surprised that she'd gotten him a new fishing vest for his trip — he'd told her he wouldn't have a spare minute for fishing. This one looked more like a safari jacket, in a shade of khaki with a good, rugged look, like it'd been cut from the earth of the Bush Country. Several pockets covered the front and offered an assortment of closures: buttons, Velcro flaps, and zippers. There were also interior pockets in both fabric and mesh, and D-rings in several places. "Does it come with its own can opener?"

"Jeff Talbot, this is for walking around the island . . . *not* for fishing trips. It'll hold maps, sunglasses, your notebook, even little antiques. Oh, and fudge. Don't forget to bring me some fudge from May's Fudge Shop."

"Fudge?"

"Uh-huh. May's is the oldest operating fudge shop in the United States, and it's on Mackinac Island."

"Should be easy enough to track down. And, honey, thanks for the vest." He laid it aside. "I'm looking forward to seeing Mackinac Island. Can you imagine a place with no cars? Just horses and bicycles and carriages everywhere. Even the taxicabs are horse-drawn. Of course, there's the *smell*, but they say you get used to it. And you have to watch where you're walking or you'll be looking for a shoe store."

He pulled her to him. "I wish you could come with me. I can't imagine the view beating what we have around here, but I've heard several people say it seems to at times. Apparently, there's a cliff just past the Grand Hotel which is lined with Victorian mansions that look out over the lake and make you feel like you're in the middle of the ocean." He stared into space, lost in a vision that he couldn't wait to turn into reality. He dragged himself back to the present and turned with a smile toward his wife. She was noticeably pale. "Honey?"

"I was okay until the ocean." Her voice was shaky.

He wrapped his arms tightly around her, wondering if he would ever get used to these sudden changes. "I didn't mean to upset you. It's just that . . ." How could he put it? "You're so well adjusted that I thought you might be getting close to . . ." Damn it. He didn't want to use the word *normal*. That would imply that he thought of her present state as abnormal.

"Sheila, I'm sorry. I didn't think. I mean, you always seem to enjoy the travel software I bring home . . ."

"I do, really. But that's because it's two-dimensional, and I'm in control. When you describe it, I *see* it, I see you there. I know it sounds crazy, but there's a difference. It's just too real when you talk about it.

"The web has opened doors for me," she continued, "and I love it. But it hasn't made the problem go away."

"Opened doors? I'm surprised you would even use those words."

"Well, it has, when you think about it. That doesn't mean I have to walk out those doors. But others can walk in, if I invite them. The world is under my roof now, on my terms. It's more than I ever expected, and it's given me a freedom I never dreamed I'd have." Sheila pulled away from her husband and smiled. "I appreciate Greer and all he's done. We're like twins — always thinking alike. When I ask him to pick up something in town, he finds exactly what I want, no matter how vague my description might be. I realize I can't function without him. But with the Internet, I've gotten back some independence. It's helped more than you'll ever know."

"I can't function without him," she'd said. Oddly, Jeff felt like the outsider, the limited one. But what was he supposed to do? He couldn't retire yet and, besides, they'd agreed it would drive them both crazy if he were home all the time. He admired his wife for her healthy outlook. At the same time, he recognized that there was a lot more to her

than he may ever learn. It was a strange, un-settling realization. He pulled Sheila back to him, held her for a long time after that. "I guess I thought your healthy attitude meant that you'd be able to go places again someday. You seem so much more open now that you're involved with things on the Internet — like visiting with people, re-searching, shopping."

"Jeff, I don't want you to hold out too much hope for that.

"That's not a sign of giving up," she has-tened to add. "Just realistic thinking."

"I realize that. But I miss the days when we traveled together. I keep hearing that Mackinac Island is perfect for couples."

She gave him a sly glance. "Just don't go looking for a replacement, Talbot."

"Not a chance, and you know it." He was irritated with himself for complaining. As usual, it had taken her edgy sense of humor to put them back on safe, level ground. He would never understand how she could take it so lightly at times.

"Jeff." She cupped his chin in her hand and gently kissed his lips. "Don't beat your-self up over my staying behind. You knew all this going in."

She stood abruptly, effectively ending their conversation, and reached for his new vest. "I want to finish your packing before dinner."

Jeff nodded, not wanting to upset Sheila

again, knowing that anything he said would come out wrong. He would've preferred to do his own packing, but he recognized his wife's need to participate. As he watched Sheila leave the room, he recalled their first months together. Sure, he had known when they married that she was agoraphobic. But her illness hadn't been nearly as advanced, as limiting as it was now. They went out several nights a week, practically gorging themselves on all that Seattle had to offer. She wouldn't go beyond the boundaries of the city, but hell, she didn't have to. The city had virtually all they could want. They attended everything from baseball games to the ballet. They made it a goal to see how many coffeehouses they could visit. She had even kept a journal, noting favorite blends, the atmosphere of her favorite haunts.

She'd enjoyed getting together with friends for lunch, going out for a weekly manicure, hopping down to Pike Place and choosing the ingredients for a new recipe she'd come up with, shopping the boutiques.

Then the changes began, subtle at first. He'd noticed that she was purchasing more and more when they went antiquing, yet the items never seemed to show up anywhere in the house. Only later did he realize that she was preparing for a life under the confines of a single roof.

She took a large portion of her trust fund

and began stockpiling for her own collections as well as for future gifts for Jeff and others in her life — others being a group that had diminished to almost no one as fewer and fewer of her friends came around.

She bought sets of china, inkwells, walking sticks. She stored up clothing, buying multiples when she found something she particularly liked. She became increasingly selective, realizing that she would no longer need black cocktail dresses and sexy high heels. She bought sweaters, jeans, slippers, pajamas.

At first, Jeff wondered how she could possibly enjoy the newly acquired treasures. It reminded him of those few clients who had set him up with bank accounts and given him carte blanche to buy up everything he could find from a specific era in order to create a particular mood for a room, or an office, or an entire home. These weren't true collectors. They simply threw money at a notion, an idea. Their hands didn't quiver with the anticipation of holding a letter written by Jack London. Their hearts never pounded against their chest walls because the item they'd searched for all their lives was finally right in front of them with a price tag attached.

He'd worried that Sheila had become one of *them*. But when she converted two adjoining bedrooms on the third floor into an antiques booth of sorts, he had understood.

Now, when she longed to go antiquing, she would dress for an "outing" and go to her surrogate store and make a purchase or two. On those days, she would have Greer pick up lunch from one of her favorite places, like Beba's or Pasta Bella's. Greer, devoted beyond duty, would play along, serving her minted iced tea and bacon quiche, and she'd lunch in the sunny breakfast room while admiring her purchases. She had the healthiest attitude about her agoraphobia of anyone Jeff had ever heard of. He attributed it to her foresight during the time in which she could still leave their home.

Jeff had expected Sheila's illness to be harder on her than on him. And it had been, in many ways, before she got caught in the web. Personally, he couldn't imagine life without travel. He loved it, thrived on it. But the two had a special relationship, an odd combination of dependence and independence. Still, he missed having her with him when he traveled. He would have loved to take her places, show her —

Damn! He'd forgotten to give her the gift he'd brought home. It took him a moment to remember where he'd left it. The dining room. He was doubling back toward the kitchen when Greer peeked around a corner.

"The missus?" he asked.

That was another thing Jeff had trouble adjusting to: hearing Greer call Sheila "the missus." Greer and Sheila shared the same birth year, nearly a decade under Jeff's.

"She's upstairs."

Without comment, Greer produced Jeff's shopping bag, then turned and went back toward the dining room.

In light of what had just happened with Sheila, Jeff questioned whether or not his choice of gifts was a wise one. But Sheila *had* mentioned it a few weeks before and, besides, he wanted to give her something before leaving.

He found her in his dressing room and handed her the unwrapped package. "I should've chosen something different this time."

"I doubt that." She took the package. By the look on her face when she recognized the colorful, weightless box, he knew he'd gotten the right item.

"You did say you wanted to explore Africa. No reason why you can't take a virtual trip while I'm in Michigan. And look at the bright side; you won't need a pith helmet."

She gave him a quick hug, then put the software aside and reviewed what she'd packed for him. "I think I've chosen the proper wardrobe for your trip. The Grand Hotel's web site really helped. Evenings are more formal, so I've included your black suit, a sport coat and slacks, several ties, and three sets of your favorite cuff links. Also, some casual stuff for exploring the island. I may have gone overboard. You're only going to be gone a couple of days."

"I'm sure it's fine," he said as he walked into their adjoining bedroom. He sat on the edge of the bed and absently rubbed the back of his neck.

"Headache?"

He nodded. Sheila crawled behind him and began massaging his shoulders. He groaned, allowing her kneading fingers to release the day's stresses. He told her about the strange confrontation with Frank Hamilton.

When he'd finished, she said, "He's lucky the old woman didn't shoot him and get it over with. You can't be too careful these days. To tell you the truth, I'm always surprised that you get into as many homes as you do."

"Thanks a lot, hon." He was surprised Sheila would even hint that someone might be leery of him.

"You know what I mean. People have to be on their guard now. They should be, at least."

"There are still a lot of smart folks out there, ones who are good judges of character." Jeff stretched his neck from side to side, amazed at how quickly the tight muscles were responding. "Hell, I'd talk to Jack the Ripper if I had a .38 stashed in my pocket."

"But you talk to strangers all the time,

with no way of knowing if one of them might be dangerous. Just because you're the solicitor doesn't mean you're the safe one." Sheila's hands worked their way down his back, making broad, firm strokes along the knotted muscles. "You don't miss carrying a gun, do you?"

"No. Not now. I did at first, but I'm not sure why. I mean, I never used the damned thing, and it got to be a nuisance having to strap it on every day. I don't know a desk jockey who ever actually shot anyone."

"You were a little more than a desk jockey. Besides, do you really think that perps stealing antiques are less likely to shoot somebody, just because they know something about pricey objects?"

He knew she was right, but he'd had enough of shop talk. "I think that your use of the word *perps* just caused dinner to be postponed." He pivoted and stretched out on the bed, drawing Sheila down with him.

She tried to pull away. "C'mon, Talbot, I need to get my apron and finish your dinner and —"

"Would you make it one of those lacy little maid's aprons?" he asked, nuzzling her neck.

She slapped at him playfully. "What would be the point? You'd have it shredded before I could say 'Coffee, tea, or me?' "

"Yeah, but the exercise would ease my stress level a hell of a lot better than a back rub."

50

"You've never complained about my strong fingers before."

"Oh, I'm not complaining. But I sure could use some attention before I go traipsing across the country."

"Your dinner might burn," she warned, but the caution held no weight. She was feverishly unbuttoning his shirt.

And that was one of the things Jeff loved most about his wife. No matter how much pride she took in her cooking, she had her priorities straight.

"What's Greer doing tonight?" Jeff watched Sheila as she put on a navy silk peignoir set he'd given her for Christmas.

"You mean after rescuing our dinner?" She threw him a sly smile. "Going to the theater. A new musical is opening tonight at the Fifth Avenue."

"Has he left yet?"

"About a half hour ago." Sheila kissed him lightly on the forehead. "I'll see you in the breakfast room in fifteen minutes."

Jeff didn't have to ask how Sheila knew that Greer had prevented a disaster in the kitchen. She had an amazing sense of everything that went on in the house. She knew who was on which of the four levels — five, if you counted the widow's walk up top. He had learned a long time ago to stop questioning her skill at this. He just figured it was

51

something she'd developed over years of never having left the premises. The house was a part of her, and she knew its movements as well as if her own motor skills were instructing it. It was an extension of her, and it seemed to Jeff that she could feel what was going on inside it, just as surely as she could feel Jeff's touch.

When Jeff first met Sheila, she was a self-taught chef and better than many who'd been professionally trained. She was working as an assistant at a Seattle restaurant whose reservation book was perpetually full. The two fell in love quickly, and married within weeks.

She had expressed an interest in pursuing professional training and becoming head chef somewhere. Eager to support her interests, Jeff had decided to send her to Cordon Bleu in Paris as a birthday gift. By the time a slot opened up, however, her illness had progressed to a new and demanding level. She couldn't bring herself to board the plane.

She was twenty-two.

They'd sought out Greer then, and life as they had known it was forever changed.

Chapter Five

"Excuse me, sir. Are you a guest of the hotel?"

Jeff turned toward the deep voice with an accent that reminded him of someplace warm and tropical. A young man with skin as dark and smooth as mahogany stood over him, dressed in an impeccably tailored white jacket and black slacks. Balanced at his shoulder was a silver tray of crystal stemware that winked in the late afternoon sun.

Jeff had sought out a far-reaching corner at the west end of the hotel's expansive porch and was stealing a moment to relax after a day packed tight with travel: first by car, then plane, then another plane, another car, a ferry, and, finally, a horse-drawn taxicab. With his feet planted firmly on the carpet of the Grand Hotel's lobby, he'd found himself thinking about the fact that he'd have all that travel to repeat, in reverse, in less than forty-eight hours.

He was enjoying the brisk autumn air that swept up from the Great Lakes, wondering how the fishing was, when he'd been asked if he was a guest of the hotel.

"Yes," he said, irritated with the interruption yet curious whether the employee was about to offer him a drink.

"Our dress code began at six, sir."

Automatically, Jeff checked his watch. Although he'd moved it forward three hours in order to allow for the change from Pacific to Eastern time, he'd completely lost track.

He looked down at his khakis and retro-print shirt with woodies, surfboards, and palm trees in muted blues and tans, then nodded to the employee and made his way to his room.

His suite — The Lord Astor, he'd been told — was located on the fourth floor and offered a "stunning view," according to the desk clerk, of the Straits of Mackinac and the five-mile-long bridge that connected Michigan's upper and lower peninsulas. The room had a navy blue color scheme and typical amenities (coffeemaker, safe, hair dryer), which were juxtaposed with an antique bedroom set — Sheraton design, he believed, although identifying furniture wasn't his strong suit. The tester bed and a straight-front chest of drawers were carved of mahogany, with well-executed detail that alluded to the fine New England work of the early 1800s. It had never been explained to Jeff just when the Latin word *testa* — "head" — had come to be applied to the canopy of a bed.

The view from his balcony was even better

than the clerk had intimated, but the room wasn't what Jeff had hoped for.

A few days earlier, he'd tried to secure the Napoleon Suite with no success. Jeff Talbot, who was not given to premonitions, had had one about the suite and believed that it would somehow assure his acquisition of Blanche's Napoleonic cabaret set.

He checked the weekend schedule and made a mental list of the festival's events he planned to attend. Friday — that was tonight — the gala preview party; Saturday morning, he'd catch a seminar or two, view the antiques slated for Sunday morning's special auction — specifically, the cabaret set — and check out the booths. Following that would be a luncheon buffet, more seminars, afternoon tea at four, then a break for everyone to get decked out for the final evening of the festival. He'd head back to Seattle immediately after Sunday's auction.

He dressed in tan slacks, a French-cuffed white shirt, and a Frank Lloyd Wright tie with the usual architectural influence in black, tan, eggplant, and sage. All this was orchestrated around a pair of vintage cuff links from his collection. Made in the 1940s, they were large oval disks of African ivory, inlaid with stalking tigers of jade with glinting amethyst eyes, all set in eighteen-karat gold.

He had a few minutes to spare, so he hung

his black sport coat on the valet and seated himself at the desk.

He took a sheet of stationery and an envelope from the leather folder. It was heavy stock, printed with a detailed etching of the hotel in reds and greens and yellows. He picked up a pen and began to write.

My Dearest Sheila,

I'll bet you thought I might forget to write you from this fabulous place, thus robbing your aptly named "Private Hotel Stationery Collection" of a treasured entry. Not a chance.

It's heaven here, or as near as I've seen (apart from The Emerald City, of course) in a very long time. The absence of vehicles, combined with the Victorian charm of this little island, has put me in an immediate state of calm. I couldn't ask for better weather, and the Great Lakes are more formidable than I'd expected. Two days here will do me more good than a month practically anywhere else.

Red geraniums are everywhere here at the Grand, from the actual plants in lattice boxes that run the length of the front porch to the ones woven into the carpets and printed on everything from the directory to the cocktail napkins. You would love it.

Although my suite isn't the one I

wanted, it's plenty comfortable. The feature I find most appealing is the balcony. I'm on the fourth floor, and the bird's eye view (as it were) reminds me a little of the one from our own widow's walk: large stretches of water, gardens bright with fall color, rooftops, church steeples, the town below. I can see the bridge, too, a five-mile-long span which connects the state's upper and lower peninsulas. Impressive.

I have good feelings about this trip and am confident that I'll be returning with Blanche's prize.

Likely, I will feel your touch before these pages do — not a complaint, I assure you. When you have read this, find me, kiss me . . .

All my love,

Jeff

Jeff put on his jacket and, feeling festive, replaced the conservative three-point pocket square with a tan flounce of silk pinstriped with sage.

He slipped a slim wallet into his breast pocket, seized his room key from the credenza — he was amazed and comforted to find that it was a real key and not a plastic credit card look-alike — and headed out the door.

He heard the elevator open, then he saw a young couple step into it and out of sight.

57

The man, tall and blond and deeply tanned, stuck his head out and told Jeff they would hold, then disappeared back inside.

Jeff picked up his pace and hurried into the waiting elevator.

The young man punched the button for the first floor. "Are you here for the antiques?"

"Yes," Jeff replied. "My first time."

"You must have been drawn here by the special auction."

"Right again. But I understand tonight there's a preview of all the booths."

The young woman laughed. "Previewing the items takes a backseat to previewing the people, Mr. — ?"

"Jeff Talbot." He thought he was watching a scene from *Breakfast at Tiffany's*. The woman wore deep red lipstick, the quintessential little black dress, large fifties-style black sunglasses, and a picture hat over her glossy black hair.

She extended her hand. "I'm Jennifer Hurst, and this is my husband, Ben. When you've attended this event for as many years as we have, you learn to check out the competition before you check out the antiques." She removed her glasses. Her brown eyes had a playful light. "Are you looking for something in particular?"

"Sweetheart," Ben said. "You're going to scare Mr. Talbot away."

"Call me Jeff. And I don't scare that easily." He smiled. "Otherwise, I wouldn't have chosen antiques as a profession."

"Profession?" Jennifer leaned in. "Are you one of the sellers?"

Jeff laughed. If he wasn't careful, this one would try to buy the gold from his teeth. "Actually, I'm a picker."

"A picker?" Ben said. "You could've fooled me."

"I get that a lot." He looked at Jennifer. "What do you collect?"

"Several things, but mostly porcelain: vases, figurines, dinnerware, tea sets. What about you?"

Jeff's heart missed a beat. Were they here for the cabaret set? There was no way he could ask. "Like I said, I'm a picker. Mostly, I find items for others —"

"Which is exactly why you shouldn't tell him what we came here for."

"Don't be silly, Ben. It's his first year here, and we know who to go to first for what we want."

The elevator door opened with a jerk, and Jennifer quickly replaced her dark glasses. As the three stepped into a flurry of animated, well-dressed people holding champagne glasses and balancing small plates of hors d'oeuvres, Ben said, "We're having dinner with a friend after the preview. Would you join us?"

Jeff liked the young couple and would welcome the company under any circumstances. Considering Jennifer's last statement, however, he was especially appreciative of the dinner invitation. He wanted to know if this pair was after the tea set, and dinner would be his best chance to do some discreet investigating. He wasn't one to use people, but he would need to be on top of things if he was going to end up with it. "I'd love to."

Chapter Six

After arranging to meet the Hursts outside the main dining room at eight, Jeff set out to locate the bartender in the crowded parlor. He succeeded, ordered a martini, and began working his way through the crowd. Most of the attendees seemed comfortable with their surroundings and with one another, and he figured there were a lot of repeat guests at the annual event. There were some as young as Ben and Jennifer Hurst. Others doddered along on canes and behind walkers, and he couldn't help but admire them. He hoped he would still be pursuing antiques thirty or forty years from now.

He stationed himself near three empty chairs and studied the people in the room. Perhaps Jennifer Hurst's prediction was right. You attended the preview to check out the competition instead of the merchandise. He caught himself idly guessing who among the group would try to outbid him for the famous cabaret set. Although it had been out of circulation for half a century, he was sure the recent buzz of its inclusion in the auction had reached several who were interested. He assumed Blanche hadn't heard because the other pickers were like him; they didn't want to get her hopes up in case something went wrong. It wasn't necessary that he concentrate on the competition. Blanche was prepared to pay whatever it took to bring the set back into her possession. But it was as good a game as any while he waited.

He was glad to see that the Little Black Dress and wide-brimmed hats weren't going out of style. Several women were wearing the traditional after-six ensemble, and Jeff wondered absently whether Ben had ever approached another woman, thinking it was Jennifer. Ben could've sneaked up from behind and planted a bear hug on any number of women and never once succeeded in embracing his own wife. Thank God it wasn't a lineup at police headquarters.

Police headquarters. Mackinac Island must have police, he thought. Jeff speculated at what sorts of tickets might be written on an island with no motorized vehicles. Can the driver of a horse-drawn wagon be ticketed for speeding? Can he be jailed for DWI? *Was* there a jail?

Jeff was picturing these odd scenarios when three elderly women made their way over and took up residence in the trio of chairs beside him. They seemed not to notice him standing there, as they were in a heated discussion about proper dress for such an event as the preview party. All three women were dressed in black and wearing hats and gloves. Two of the ladies had walking sticks — antique sticks, he noted — and he tried to get a closer look without seeming obtrusive.

Both sticks were made of ebony, but the handles were different. The one held by the woman at the far end was almost identical to one in his own collection: ivory, carved into the shape of a burlesque dancer's leg bent at the knee to provide a long, slender handle. It was likely from the Victorian era, when risqué subjects were a highly popular counterpoint to the prudish ways impressed upon society by Queen Victoria. Check any time of repression and you'll find the seedy, scandalous objects of a counterculture.

It made sense that the woman in the far chair was using a man's walking stick. With her height and build, she would need the length and security a more substantial stick offered.

The other woman's walking stick depicted an eagle's talons clutching a glass orb. The talons were sterling silver, as was the collar, or band, that joined the handle to the cane. On both canes, the ferrules had been replaced with practical rubber tips.

Jeff figured that the ladies' antique canes would each bring four figures at auction. He'd seen historically valuable pieces — those that had belonged to former U.S. presidents or British aristocracy — fetch more than ten grand.

After Jeff secretly admired the women's walking sticks, he realized what a strain the situation must put on the third woman. The tiny thing, whose skin and eyes were nearly as blue white as her hair, was seated between the other two. Likely, she'd been stationed conveniently in the middle so that she could be of assistance to either of the others when they needed it. She would be expected to hold doors open, pick up dropped canes, and retrieve canes left behind in restaurants or hanging on shopping carts (much as they declared needing them, cane users were always leaving the artificial appendages somewhere). In spite of this extra burden, she seemed to be enjoying herself. She wore a smile of anticipation, of someone who waited for exciting things to happen around her.

As Jeff listened to the three females talk, he couldn't help but be reminded of *Steel Magnolias*. They were what Clairee, M'Lynn, and Ouizer would be like in another thirty years: sharp-witted and still not willing to take any crap off anybody.

He grinned when the woman closest to him, in her whiskey-smooth Southern drawl, made a remark about a man's salmon-colored jacket. Instinctively, Jeff looked at the man in question.

Something cuffed Jeff's shin. Startled, he jumped.

"You agree with me, don't you, young man?" The woman nearest him had reached out and tapped him with her cane.

She looked a little younger than her companions, although her light brown hair was heavily shot with gray. Her hazel eyes still sparked and hadn't yet begun to cloud like so many older people's did.

Jeff couldn't remember the last time he'd been called a young man. Everything was relative, he supposed. The old woman winked. He grinned, then looked at the man in question. "It does stand out in the crowd, doesn't it?"

"Black after six, as simple as sticks," said the woman in the middle.

"Now, Ruth Ann, I don't know as I agree with you." This came from the large lady at the opposite end. She was black, with dark, supple skin. Her black dress had an ivory panel running the length of it from neckline to floor, and her lipstick and huge disk earrings were the same vibrant orange. She put Jeff in mind of a king penguin. "A little color makes for individuality."

"Well, Asia, we can always count on you for that." The woman who had cuffed Jeff's shin rolled her eyes.

"Now, we're from New Orleans," the one called Ruth Ann said, pronouncing it

65

N'awlins, "and you don't necessarily *have* to wear black after six down there. Lord, we'd probably have more people a dyin' of the heat stroke than *we* would of old age. But *we* know enough to wear black when the function calls for it, don't we, girls?"

"That's right," said one.

"Yes, indeed," added the other.

"Where are our manners?" said the woman nearest Jeff. "I'm Lily Chastain. This is Ruth Ann Longan, and down there is Asia Graham."

"My pleasure, ladies." He was drawn in by their Southern charm and when each offered her hand in the manner requiring a kiss and not a shake, he willingly obliged. With a bow, he introduced himself.

"Just like a true gentleman," Ruth Ann said, sighing contentedly.

"Is this your first time here?" asked Asia. "I'd like to think we would've remembered you if you had attended the festival before."

"Yes, ma'am, it is. I arrived just today from Seattle, and I'm beginning to think I'm the only new face here."

"Well, you won't want to miss it again," said Ruth Ann. "It's quite the to-do."

"Yes," added Lily, "and our most anticipated trip of the year. Isn't it, girls?"

Asia and Ruth Ann chimed their agreement.

"Then, Miz Chastain, I'll have to put it on

my schedule for next year."

"Please," said Lily, "call us by our first names, would you? So many people say Miz this and Ma'am that. Why, I'm afraid sometimes that we're going to forget what our given names are, for heaven's sake."

"Not likely, *Miz* Lily," Asia said. "You've got that damned brooch the size of Shreveport pinned to your front porch to remind you." Asia rolled her eyes. "Lily collects anything and everything lily of the valley."

"Don't get ugly, Asia," Lily said. "It's really no different from why you collect your stuff." She gazed up at Jeff. "It's for my *name*, don't you know?"

"Good reason," Jeff assured. "Be careful what you buy these days. I understand someone's reproducing an inkwell with a lily of the valley design. I'd hate to see you lose a few hundred dollars to some shyster."

"Why, thank you, young man. I swan, it's getting more and more challenging to determine what's real and what isn't, and I certainly don't want to buy anything new. My father always wanted everything new and shiny, said things that had been used by others should be thrown out with the dishwater."

"I'm afraid lots of people feel that way." Nearby, someone vacated a chair. Jeff pulled it over and sat down. "You can't get the thrill of collecting across to anyone who doesn't collect *something*. It helps to learn if a person collects things still being produced, like baseball cards or Hot Wheels or" — Jeff clenched his jaw — "even Beanie Babies. Then we can appeal to their sense of acquisition."

"Sounds like you feel the same way I do about those things — Beanie Babies." This was Asia again. Jeff liked her way of cutting to the core. "Ruth Ann wondered if she should start grabbin' those up — Ruth Ann collects bears and dolls and such — but I told her she was a fool if she did."

"That don't mean you're right, Asia," said Ruth Ann.

"Ruthie, by the time those things have any value — if they ever do — we'll be long dead and buried. I say spend your money on something from way back, something with a *past*." Asia gave her head one determined nod, then made a noise that indicated the subject was closed.

Ruth Ann pouted but didn't offer a rebuttal.

Jeff felt sorry for the tiny woman, but he was afraid to address her for fear she'd start crying. He directed the conversation elsewhere. "What do you collect, Asia?"

"Black history — African-American, if you're politically correct, which I ain't. Not that it ever surprises anyone. The collection part, not the PC. But it did start on a personal level. When I was ten years old — a very impressionable age, mind you — my grandmother presented me with the slave tags of her maternal grandparents." Asia paused. "Do you know what slave tags are?"

Jeff said he'd heard of them, but the woman commenced explaining anyway.

"To boil it down, slave owners had to pay a tax and register their slaves. The tag had an ID number to match the town treasurer's records — the town usually bein' Charleston — and listed the slave's work: porter, servant, blacksmith, and so on. There are a lot of fake tags being made nowadays.

"Anyhow, I became obsessed with our culture, readin' and collectin' everything I could get my hands on. Back then, a lot of people didn't want the stuff, so they'd just bring it to me."

"Asia's got one of the largest black memorabilia collections in the United States," Ruth Ann boasted. "Even Ray Charles has been to her home to see it."

Ruth Ann's sudden change took Jeff by surprise.

Asia leaned toward Jeff. "Course you know he can't see." She said it low, like it was a big secret.

Jeff acknowledged that, yes, he knew.

Asia fell back in her chair and continued. "He'd heard about the hangin's, though, felt drawn to come down to —"

"Hangings?" Jeff snapped backward as if he'd been hit.

"I guess you don't see much of the stuff up — wait a minute. You thought I meant real hangin's? Lord no, child! *Photographs* of hangin's. God knows they're real enough, though."

Jeff felt only marginally better. Still, he had to confess that he didn't know what the woman was talking about. He told her so.

"You've read about how in the Old West, everybody would go to town and gather round to watch the lynchin's? Well, they did it in the Old South, too. Only not near that long ago. Photographers took pictures of the black folk a hangin' there. Not just of men, neither. Women, half-grown kids. Made post-cards out of them, postcards people sent through the mail, just like you'd send a card from Mount Rushmore. Till the Postal Service banned them, that is."

It gave Jeff a chill. He wondered how the hell it was he'd never heard of these pictures, never come across any of them. "How can you stand to look at something like that?"

"Couldn't, in the beginning. First time I saw one, I had nightmares for months. I was about twelve then. There was one in some of that stuff people brought me. After that initial fright, though, I felt it was my duty to make people aware of what had been done to us.

"If you're ever in New Orleans, I'd be happy to show you my collection. It takes up most of my home."

"There you go, Asia," Lily said, "invitin' strangers to your home. Not that you're not trustworthy, young man," she hastened to add, "but we keep tellin' her she needs to be more careful."

Asia waved off her companion and Jeff seized the opportunity to steer the conversation in a different direction.

He turned to Ruth Ann and asked about her collections.

"Dolls and teddy bears, mostly," she said. "And those little muffin pans and rolling pins. All the things we couldn't afford when I was a little girl."

"Any Steiffs tucked away in that collection?"

"Two or three dozen, I suppose," Ruth Ann said distractedly. She'd seemed more fascinated with Asia's things than with her own.

Jeff speculated that the Steiff bears alone — depending on condition and rarity — were valued in the six figures. He'd learned their history from his Auntie Pim and, following the instructions in her will, had sold her collection and donated the profits to a children's charity.

The German-made bears got a real boost in the United States when Teddy Roosevelt refused to kill a bear cub while on a hunting trip. That act drastically increased the demand for Margarete Steiff's button-in-ear creations, and teddy bears were put on the map.

Conversation with the three women had been overwhelming, like walking into an antique mall and not knowing where to begin. Jeff needed some air.

He stood. "Ladies, I hope I have the pleasure of visiting with you again this weekend. If you'll excuse me, I'd like to take another stroll down the porch."

"Oh, refer to it as a veranda, dear," Lily said. "It's so much more soothing a word than *porch*. Don't you agree?" She smiled warmly.

"You're absolutely right, Lily."

Jeff bowed. Southerners do have a way with their words.

Chapter Seven

Jeff went out onto the porch — *veranda* — but it was as crowded with people as the Parlor. He descended the stairs and crossed the narrow, paved path that separated the hotel from the sprawling grounds below. An arched passageway, nearly concealed by foliage, led to the gardens and pool. He descended more steps and stopped on a small landing. Stretching before him was a large expanse of manicured green, bordered with several carefully tended flower beds. Trees whose leaves were turning colors, giving a texture and depth not seen in summer, showcased a large stone fountain. Actually, there were a dozen or so fountains: a large center one with several more around the perimeter of the pond, the water gushing from stylized shells.

To his right, more steps led down to a concrete walkway that was lined with streetlamps. If he recalled the guide map correctly, the walkway led to the swimming pool. It was named after Esther Williams, according to the information accompanying photographs he'd seen in the hotel's corridors, as it had been used in the making of her 1947 film, *This Time for Keeps*. Another film had been shot on location at the Grand, and Jeff found it interesting that both had the word *time* in them. Fitting, for an island that maintains its Victorian charm from another era. Jane Seymour, who'd gone on to act in a western series, had fared better with horses than Christopher Reeve in the years since they'd starred in *Somewhere in Time*. This second movie to be shot at the Grand Hotel was filmed about thirty years after the Williams flick. It was a shame Reeve couldn't go back in time now, and stay away from horses.

A small group of swimmers, wrapped in towels and walking briskly, made their way up from the pool area, darted up the steps, and disappeared behind him. On a bench near the fountain sat a couple romantically entwined and oblivious to the world. Jeff felt a twinge of envy.

Suddenly, from directly below him, Jeff heard a voice — gravelly, angry — as it chastised someone for leaving hedge clippers in the garden. The answering voice was young and filled with a sullen attitude, using words like *dude* and *chill, man.*

Jeff figured the kid had dreamed of a cushy summer job. He probably expected to make enough money for some new wheels and still have plenty of time off to pursue tanned beach bunnies. Jeff had been that way himself and liked to think it wasn't that long ago. He smiled as he climbed the stairs and headed back to the hotel.

The Gallery was just off the Parlor, with a short, wide staircase leading to the Conference Center. Jeff arrived just as the ribbon-cutting ceremony was starting. This kicked off the preview party. There was such a press of people, however, that he really couldn't see anything. After the cutting, an official with the festival invited the guests to visit the booths. Purchases could be made at this time. Jeff went in the opposite direction. This land-rush approach didn't fit his idea of antiquing and, besides, he'd confirmed that the cabaret set was to be in Sunday's auction.

He made his way to the Geranium Bar, where he ordered a martini and stationed himself at one of the large plate glass windows to take in the view of the Straits.

He had a few minutes before his dinner companions were due to arrive. Although he enjoyed meeting new people, he could only take them in small doses. He was used to spending a lot of time alone, driving the region around Seattle, hunting down places that looked promising for finding loot. He nursed the martini. The evening promised a lot more liquor and he wanted to pace himself.

He finished his drink and left the bar. He

got only a short distance down the corridor when he saw the Hursts approaching. He stopped. With them was a man so large that the young couple looked like a pair of candlesticks flanking Buckingham Palace.

Jeff had seen photos of the man. *Photo,* he corrected, because the same black and white head shot always accompanied the man's articles that were frequently published in the trades. In it was the white hair, the bushy mustache, the portly jowls. The photo had been taken several years before, Jeff now observed. The hair had obviously gone silver early in the man's life, and he was heavier now. Also, the photo had given no indication of his massive height. He could've checked the top of a highboy for dust without so much as straining his ample neck.

Ben Hurst hadn't mentioned that their dinner companion was Edward Davenport, the most sought-after auctioneer between America's two coasts.

Davenport wore an expertly tailored black tuxedo, generously cut to accommodate his bulk. His vest, bow tie, and pocket square were of royal blue brocaded satin that enhanced his sapphire eyes. As the man drew closer, Jeff wondered if it might actually be the other way around, and the shimmery fabric was picking up its hue from the intensely blue eyes.

Jennifer spotted Jeff and smiled. He

nodded, returned the gesture. Ben and the auctioneer were deep in conversation, walking and talking without being aware of anything or anyone around them. Jeff didn't envy the type, but he did find their way of gliding through life, seemingly untouched, somehow appealing. They walked along, oblivious to their surroundings, confident in some inner homing device that assured they would always arrive intact at their destination. They never tripped, or ran into things, or ended up lost. Everything was waiting for them when they arrived, as they believed it should be. Some — those who appeared to take this gift for granted — truly believed that life was supposed to work this way. They neither questioned it nor tried to explain their ability to utilize it.

A second species consciously strove for this sort of existence, and those belonging to that group were usually pains in the neck. They abused their gift.

Jeff belonged in another category entirely, a third one, whose members paid attention, planned ahead, watched for exits, rechecked tickets, double-checked reservations. They were always running into snags, waiting in lines, and being put on hold, in spite of their concentrated efforts to avoid all such problems. Jeff had learned to accept his fate long ago, thus allowing extra time for damn near everything.

Jennifer touched her husband's arm slightly,

subtly. Without missing a beat or allowing his conversation with his guest to be interrupted, he reached into his breast pocket, withdrew two small red booklets, and flashed them to the hostess at the podium. Simultaneously, Davenport did the same. Jeff recognized the booklets as those that served as guest identification; he retrieved his from his pocket and joined the three at the podium.

Jennifer took Jeff by the arm, pulled him into the fold.

Ben extended his hand. Jeff grasped it firmly and said, "This little book is more valuable than I thought."

Ben laughed. "Jennifer has threatened to keep these little treasures in the pocket of her pajamas in case we're evacuated because of fire. She's afraid she won't be able to get back inside without it."

"That's nonsense, Benjamin Hurst. You know I don't wear pajamas." Jennifer looked directly at Jeff as she delivered the line.

Jeff smiled and glanced at Davenport, who was blushing.

Ben didn't react one way or the other. "Allow me to introduce you to one of the best auctioneers in the country. Edward Davenport, Jeffrey Talbot."

"*The* best, from what I've heard." Jeff extended his hand. "An honor. I recognized you as soon as I spotted the three of you approaching."

Davenport took his hand. Jeff had experienced more action from a dead trout.

"Have we met?" the auctioneer said.

"No, but I've read several of your articles on antiques. It's good to finally meet you in color."

"I wish they would burn that bloody photo. The publishers could use anyone's mug, and most readers wouldn't be the wiser." The man spoke slowly and in low, soft tones. The last thing anyone might have guessed him to be was an auctioneer. "And what's all the fuss about my articles? If another person trots out that line tonight, I shall go back to the queen."

"Edward, stop teasing." Jennifer laughed nervously, then turned to Jeff and said by way of explanation, "Several people have commented on his photograph today."

As they started toward the dining room, Jeff entertained the notion of going to his own room and having dinner brought up.

The maître d' ushered them to a reserved table by the windows. Jeff stood for a long moment, taking in the wild yellows, oranges, greens, and pinks that colored the room. Partway down the expanse, an orchestra played a jazzy Duke Ellington number — "In The Mood," if memory served. Jeff could barely see the band members and wondered offhandedly if binoculars were on the menu.

Moonlight shone across the lake, and beyond that the tiny flicker of headlights could be seen moving across Mackinac Bridge. The bridge itself was strung with sparkling lights, giving it a skeletal effect.

The sommelier approached their table, followed by a white-jacketed waiter carrying an ice bucket and a stand. Both men were Jamaican. "Champagne." The sommelier displayed the label to the auctioneer. "Compliments of the Mussers."

"Please thank them for me," Davenport said, then turned to the group. "The owners," he said. "Grand people."

Jeff started to remark on Davenport's pun, but the auctioneer didn't seem to notice that he'd made one. Jeff kept quiet.

"To each his own," Davenport said. He tipped back his glass.

Jeff had expected something more eloquent in the way of a toast.

When the waiter returned for their orders, Jeff listened as his companions requested intriguingly named dishes such as Green Tea Smoked Mahimahi Filet and Tomato and Truffle Bisque with Fried Onion Petals. He felt a pang of regret that Sheila wasn't there to enjoy the elaborate menu.

He'd called her when he had first arrived at the hotel to let her know he had made it safely. They'd agreed not to talk again until the next afternoon but, after seeing the impressive dinner menu, he knew he'd have to call her sooner with a full report.

When his turn came, he played it safe with the salad and soup courses — greens with pine nuts and goat cheese, and a minestrone — but branched out with an appetizer called Vodka-Cured Salmon with Chevre Dressing (any combination of fish and alcohol was worth trying in Jeff's estimation) and an entrée of Slow-Roasted Duck Breast with Blackberry-Plum Sauce. He hoped the taste would live up to the creative titles. A Vegetable Napoleon was on the menu, but he passed it over. Not a damn one of his premonitions had done him any good so far.

After they'd ordered, Jennifer announced, "Edward was Carleton's first choice when they decided to have a special auction this year."

Carleton. It took Jeff a moment to realize she meant Carleton Varney, the man responsible for the interior decoration of the hotel and the reigning talent behind the Antiques Festival. Varney's unique touch even graced rooms in the White House. Jeff wondered if the Hursts were really on a first-name basis with the icon.

"Will Carleton Varney be here?"

"Didn't you see him at the Gala Preview?" asked Jennifer. "Everyone gathered in the Gallery while Carleton held a little ribbon-cutting ceremony. Then we all walked through for a peek at the treasures."

"Just a peek? Or, did the vendors actually start sales then?"

"It's a short weekend," said Ben. "No one misses the chance to move merchandise. Carleton walked through, said a few things about the weekend. As usual, he picked up an item here and there, then put it back down and moved on. Within seconds, people swarmed the table, trying to buy the Midas-touched object."

The appetizers came, and Davenport inhaled his before the others could determine whether the elaborate concoctions on their plates matched the menu's descriptions of what they'd ordered. Then he popped a pink capsule-shaped tablet into his mouth and washed it down with champagne. The investigator in Jeff wondered what it was. "So, Talbot, what is it you're after this weekend?"

It was an interesting way to phrase a question. The auctioneer put Jeff on edge. "You'll find out when you drop your gavel, and my name's behind it."

"Ah, a clandestine approach."

"Jeff is a picker, Edward," offered Jennifer.

"A picker. Shouldn't you be out rummaging through someone's attic?"

"Some people think 'picker' is just another word for bum. Chances are, I'll make more this weekend than you do."

Before the auctioneer could respond, Ben cleared his throat and said, "You know, Jeff, we didn't have time earlier to ask what you collect."

Jeff decided to ignore the puffed-up auctioneer. "More things than I should, probably: walking sticks, cuff links, silver. And I'm always picking up things for my — for some other collectors. Inkwells, porcelains, just about anything Victorian." He'd almost said *wife*. The decision to keep Sheila a secret had been a necessary one, but he often wondered whether it was wise. However, trying to explain her illness had become increasingly complicated. Even friends who knew about it became less and less understanding as the Talbots repeatedly turned down invitations. They had made the decision together, and he would try to stick to it.

"Porcelains?" Ben concentrated on his entrée. "Then we'll be bidding against one another. We have our sights locked in on several auction pieces."

"There is plenty to go around, my friends," said Davenport as he polished off his plate. Jeff thought of a political cartoon in which the government smiles at you while it's filching your last slice of bread.

His sales pitch is next, Jeff thought. He braced himself. The cabaret set would be top of the list, and he didn't want to tip his hand. Oddly, Edward Davenport didn't seize the opening. Jeff could understand the Hursts keeping quiet, but Davenport? Shouldn't he

83

be talking it up, creating more interest? Well, he figured, there were all kinds of auctioneers, just as there were all kinds of pickers.

"So, Talbot, you sit at home and read *all* my articles, but you've never been to one of my auctions? I find that rather odd." Davenport sat back in his chair and clasped his hands around his bulging waist.

Jeff bristled. When he'd commented on the articles earlier, it was not as a device for endearing himself to the auctioneer, and he resented the Englishman's attitude, suggesting it. When his antiques subscriptions arrived, Jeff closed himself up in his study with the publications and a drink — Fosters in warm weather, liquor-laced coffee in cold — and devoured the latest news in the antique world. They kept him on top of the game, gave him a look at what was bringing how much, told him how much he should spend and what he could expect to profit. Sheila's subscription to *Victoria* helped, too, and she frequently marked articles for him about antiques. The publication was a good barometer for trends in antiques, as well as revealing what was being reproduced.

Jeff debated what approach to take with the auctioneer. The last thing he needed was to have this man against him, the man who practically controlled the fate of the tea set. But the older Jeff got, the more inclined he was toward intolerance.

The hell with it. He didn't go to many auctions, but that didn't mean he couldn't hold his own. He looked at Davenport evenly. "You doubt my sincerity. Given your reputation, some people may understand that, even expect it. I'm not one of them. It doesn't make sense that you aren't talking up the game, but that's beside the point. I'm here to play ball, Mr. Davenport. If you want to make it hardball, then knock yourself out. I can handle it. But I'm sure as hell not here to waste my time blowing smoke up the umpire's skirt."

Jeff considered leaving, then decided against it. He'd been looking forward to a cup of coffee at the end of the meal and, by God, he was going to have it. The hell with the English and their damned tea.

"At long bloody last!" Davenport slapped the table, setting the china and silver to rattling. His blue eyes sparked, and he gave Jeff an unmistakable look of true admiration. "Do you want to know what my day has consisted of? One very long line of pretentious people bombarding me, fawning over my work, vying for my attention, name-dropping. I pegged you for a sharp wit upon which to entertain myself. Good choice, too, I might add. You have an intelligent look about you, Talbot.

"My brain was going numb," Davenport continued. "I needed some stimulation. Don't hold it against me. If you want to know the truth, I'd just as soon have no attention at all as to have to deal with it all. Interesting, isn't it? Do a bad job, and everyone knows you. Do a good job, and you have to deal with the same thing."

It was the strangest compliment Jeff had ever received. He had to laugh. "You're in the wrong line of work for someone who doesn't like the limelight."

"True enough, Talbot, true enough. And you know what? I have no idea how I got here." He paused. "You're not angry?"

"Stunned is more like it." Actually, Jeff wasn't sure how he felt.

The waiter brought coffee and asked for dessert orders.

"I feel so much better," said the auctioneer, "I think I'll indulge and have two. Bring a slice of that cheesecake with caramel sauce, and something chocolate — I don't care what it is."

As the others were ordering dessert, a desk clerk approached and handed Davenport a sealed note. He ripped open the envelope, and his jaw clenched while he quickly read the paper. After a moment he said, "There appears to be a discrepancy with one of the lots. I hope you'll forgive me." He heaved himself from the chair and said to the waiter, "Have my desserts sent up to my room in half an hour."

"No rest for the wicked, Edward," Jennifer said.

If the auctioneer heard the snide comment, he didn't show it. He slapped the note against his palm and left.

Ben smiled at Jeff. "I hope he didn't get under your skin too much. He can be a strange one. But he's also the most intelligent man I've ever met. He's not a Ph.D. or Rhodes scholar, but I'd put his vast knowledge up against anyone who is." He sat back as their desserts came.

"Well," said Jennifer, "I think he got a little carried away this time."

"Don't take it personally, sweetheart. I think he spends so much time alone with his nose buried in history books that when he gets in a crowd, it wears on his nerves."

"I don't doubt he's intelligent." Jeff took a bite of his bread pudding with rum sauce. "I've drawn from the man's knowledge many times when I've been in the field. No one is an expert in every facet of antiques. But people like Davenport keep us from making costly mistakes."

"What kinds of mistakes?" Jennifer was trying to break a dark chocolate wafer with her spoon. She only succeeded in smearing its etching of the hotel's trademark horse and carriage.

"The biggest problem I see now is with fakes. Of course, if you're checking the antique malls, it's easy enough to walk through and spot them. I always question the authenticity of something you never used to find anywhere and suddenly it's in every fourth booth."

Ben said, "We rarely go to the malls. There are pickers who know what we're looking for, so we just leave it to them to find the stuff. Except, of course, for our annual trip here. That's because Jennifer's parents brought her to the Grand every summer when she was a little girl."

Jeff debated whether to tell them what they were missing. Of course, if everyone were as obsessed with the hunt as he was, he'd be out of business. He opted, instead, for the business approach. "If you'd like to provide me with a list before we leave this weekend, I'd be happy to watch for your items. And I can give you references, if you'd like."

"A reference isn't necessary, Talbot," said Ben. He thought for a moment. "You could keep an eye out for sports memorabilia, mainly —"

"Yes!" Jennifer interrupted, "and vintage purses — all kinds but especially the beaded ones — and sugar shakers and Fabergé eggs and cameo pins."

Jeff scrambled for his notebook.

"Oh!" She continued. "Didn't I tell you earlier I collect porcelains? Place settings, figurines, vases, chocolate sets, tea sets —"

"Jennifer welcomes any and all help in spending her inheritance."

Jennifer laughed a delicate, music box laugh, but Jeff could see in her eyes that her husband hadn't been joking.

Chapter Eight

Lightning flashed briefly, silently, along the western horizon.

The barmaid placed Jeff's brandy on the table, and he noticed that her long nails were polished to match the red geraniums encased in clear lacquer on the tabletop. She placed his printed bar tab on the table, then walked toward a man and woman in the opposite corner. They were the only other customers, and he would have thought of them as a couple, except had they been a couple, they would've taken their increasingly erotic mating dance to a room. Jeff averted his gaze and stared into his glass. He hoped this last round would induce sleep.

The Cupola Bar was a two-level lounge at the top of the hotel. Three of its four sides were glass, offering a panoramic view of the lakes. Jeff was on the upper level, which was actually a gallery with a rail to keep the tipsy from tumbling through the square opening and into the lower level. If anyone did take the plunge, he would take with him an eight-foot glass chandelier that descended out of sight through the opening.

While he drank, Jeff thought about the events of the evening. After finishing dinner with the Hursts, he had gone to The Terrace Room to check out the band and have an after-dinner drink. But it was crowded and noisy, and the sight of all those couples dancing had only served to make him miss Sheila. He'd gone back to his room and called her.

After he'd reported every detail about his dinner and the people he'd met, Sheila had said, "To tell you the truth, I don't know which sounds more eccentric."

"Eccentric or not, I'll have my work cut out for me if Jennifer Hurst is bidding for the cabaret set."

"It'll keep your skills sharp." Sheila sighed. "So, what's on your interesting agenda for the rest of the evening?"

"A movie, probably. The hotel's showing *An Affair to Remember*." He never went out to movies back home, opting instead to rent videos so that he and Sheila could watch them together. "I wish you could be here."

"Well, I can't, so let's not talk about it."

"Why can't we talk about it? I miss you, damn it."

"Let's just change the subject, okay?"

Jeff grudgingly agreed, not wanting to get in a fight long-distance. They talked about inconsequential things and rang off on a note of mutual dissatisfaction.

That's when Jeff had headed downstairs to kill a couple more hours in what he suspected would be a long evening.

No longer in the mood for a movie, he headed back upstairs to find the bar. He'd been told that the Cupola was only one flight up from his room.

Rain pelted the glass behind him. Brandy and rain: There was a combination that should help him sleep. Jeff drank slowly. He thought about asking if it was Napoleon brandy, but didn't. He was beginning to resent this inner voice that encouraged premonitions.

"A porcelain for your thoughts."

Jeff jumped, then stood and smiled. It was Jennifer. "My thoughts aren't worth that much, but I'd guess you have plenty of pieces to spare." He held a chair for her.

"Too many, probably. I've had to hire someone to come in and help me dust every week."

"I do the same thing."

"See? You need a wife to do that for you."

"You're a wife. Besides, I could have two wives and they couldn't keep up. I have an ancestor who was a lumber baron. My home has more rooms than a military funeral has guns. Some people might say I inherited a white elephant, but I wouldn't trade it for anything." Jeff took a drink. "Where's Ben?"

"He stopped to say hello to some friends."

She motioned toward the opposite corner, then smiled flirtatiously. "Were you afraid I'd hunted you down alone? No wonder you're still single. You're too skittish. You need to relax."

"I'm afraid if I do, you'll start undressing me."

"Well, not *here*." She smiled and sat back. "I'm only having fun, and probably way too much to drink." As if mentioning drink reminded her that she had one, she sipped something blue from a martini glass. "You're safe with me, Jeff. Although I do have an older sister —"

"What's going on over here?" Ben pulled up a chair.

"I was just telling Jeff about Meagan," she said with a look toward Jeff.

"Meagan? Hell, Jennifer, she wouldn't know a Model T from a Yugo. What would they have to talk about?"

"I suppose you're right, sweetheart. It was just a thought." She gave Jeff a nervous glance. "I think I'll go powder my nose."

"We need to turn in soon, anyway," Ben said. "Lots of ground to cover tomorrow."

Jennifer stood. "You're right. Let's just meet back in the room in a few minutes, okay?" She leaned over and gave her husband a long kiss, then told Jeff good night and strolled toward the stairs.

Jeff wasn't sleepy yet, and he hoped Ben

would stay a little longer and visit. There was one sure way to make that happen. "Ben, tell me more about your sports collection."

True to the collector temperament, Ben began talking about his baseball cards and autographed pigskins and pennants. He told about his favorite find and his best deal and the one that got away, stories that Jeff had heard many times from many people. The items were different, but not the people or the passions.

The barmaid announced last call.

Ben glanced at his watch. "Jennifer's probably given up on me." He rose and told Jeff good night.

After Ben left, Jeff turned his attention to the window. The rain had almost stopped, but the lightning still flashed, saying it wasn't through trying to stir up things.

Something in the gardens below caught his eye. Someone was there — a man — at the foot of the stairs by the lighted walk that led to the swimming pool. It seemed quite late for a stroll in the gardens. But the streetlamps were still burning, casting small beams of light across the walkway, and Jeff supposed the guy didn't mind getting wet.

Jeff tried to get a closer look. It appeared the man was talking with someone, although Jeff couldn't see the other person because of the overhang of foliage. Something about the man seemed familiar, and Jeff searched his mind for who it was. The brandy had begun to take effect, however, and all the people he'd met during the course of the evening began to mix in his brain.

As the conversation continued, the man seemed to become more aggressive. He paced back and forth, like an irritated coach on the sidelines, again tweaking Jeff's memory, but he still couldn't place who it was. Then the hidden party stepped forward quickly and back again. From Jeff's vantage point high above, he caught only a glimpse.

But it was enough of a glimpse to tell him that it was a woman. A woman wearing a large hat and what looked like a black dress. The hat's wide brim shielded most of her body from Jeff's view.

Just then, the man popped his forehead with the heel of his left hand. Only one man had a gesture like that. The man arguing with the woman was Frank Hamilton.

Chapter Nine

There wasn't enough brandy on the island to put Jeff to sleep after what he'd seen. What the hell was Frank Hamilton doing here, anyway? The thought of the young picker being there gnawed at Jeff, churned the brandy in his gut, took the shine off his trip.

He left the bar, double-timed the stairs, and headed for the elevator. Go to the source of aggravation, he thought, as he punched the Down button. Confront Hamilton. Tell the bastard that he had no right being at the Antiques Festival. This was — what? — a private party. No. Off limits to unethical characters? No again.

As the doors slid open, Jeff stood there and realized how stupid he was acting. Hamilton's childish *I was here first* remark from the roadside the day before rang in his ears.

And what about the woman? She was obviously talking to Frank willingly. Frank didn't have an arm hold on her or a gun pointed at her. The fact was, it didn't matter how much Jeff despised the man, there wasn't a thing he could do about his presence at a public event.

Damn. Jeff watched the doors slide shut, then made his way to his room.

It made sense, he supposed, that Frank would attend. He was, after all, in the antique business as well. Strange, though, to have seen him only yesterday in Seattle — a yesterday that seemed more like ten years ago. Now, here he was on Mackinac Island, a world removed from Seattle, Washington.

Jeff undressed and crawled into bed. He tried to sleep, but his imagination conjured up one stressful scenario after another. What if Frank had learned that Jeff was here for the cabaret set? Blanche owned All Things Old several years before Jeff had gotten into the antique business. He supposed there was no way of knowing just how many people she had put on the trail.

Jeff wondered if Frank might allude to his "secret life," as he'd also done the day before. Jeff was pretty sure that Frank didn't know about Sheila. Otherwise, why would he continue to make it sound like Jeff was hiding some deep, dark secret?

He tried to gain control of his thoughts. *If* Hamilton knew about Blanche's quest, then what? Blanche probably hadn't ever thought that the treasure she sought might show up in an auction. If more than one person was bidding for it — for *her* — then she would actually be bidding against herself. One thing was certain: Blanche was a savvy business-

97

woman. No, Jeff decided, Blanche hadn't heard about the cabaret set being here.

But anyone who knew how much she wanted it also knew that she was willing to pay anything to get it back. It was rightfully hers but, because it had been legally — if not ethically — sold by her father, she was going to have to purchase it outright. The letter of provenance didn't change that fact. If Frank got his hands on the cabaret set, he'd soak the poor woman for all she had.

If he got his hands on it. Well. He would have to make sure Frank didn't make the winning bid. Jeff was still prepared to pay anything. The young picker's presence didn't change that.

He toyed with the idea of calling Blanche and asking her how many people knew of her search. But he'd tried to keep his latest information about the cabaret set under wraps, just in case it didn't pan out, and he was relatively sure she didn't suspect his real reason for coming here.

Finally, he surmised, his best tack would be to avoid Hamilton altogether. Pretend he wasn't there and not let him know how much he got under his skin.

That decided, Jeff stopped tossing and turning. The seminars he wanted to attend would be starting in a few hours, and he needed to get some rest.

Chapter Ten

Gray slices of light outlined the heavy drapes as the first signs of dawn touched Mackinac Island. Jeff had crawled wearily from bed an hour earlier, pulled a robe over his body, and brewed a pot of his personal coffee blend — a dark-roasted mix of Colombian, Kona, and Turkish beans — that Sheila had packed for him.

The rustle he'd heard at his door earlier turned out to be a pleasant surprise of the *New York Times* in an interesting, miniature form — a sampling of articles faxed straight from the Big Apple and into the hands of the hotel's guests — via the efforts of no telling how many employees who copied and stapled and delivered it at four in the morning. It was accompanied by an impressively organized schedule of the day's events at the hotel.

Jeff had had his first cup of coffee while going over current and future events, then had showered and dressed. Now that dawn was breaking, he poured a second cup and took it onto his balcony.

The furniture was coated with water — either from last night's rain, or this morning's dew, or both — so he stood at the railing, feeling as if he were trying to see the hotel's gardens and Lake Huron through a scrim. He savored this time of morning, loved to study the changes in the landscape that took place like the *click-shink, click-shink* of a slide show.

The air smelled damp, and the rains had stirred the lake's waters, bringing up a slight fishy smell like that he'd grown up with on the Pacific Coast.

The gray dawn grew lighter with each frame, the flowers and grass and water taking on increasing degrees of warmth. Their vivid colors sharpened, revealed more detail.

He heard hooves strike pavement in the distance. The *clop, clop* reverberated, carried farther in the fog.

He strained to see as far as the fountain, but it wasn't yet visible. He drank his coffee and watched silently as the fog slowly burned off.

Specks of color began showing around the hazy perimeter as blooms of goldenrod, purple coneflower, asters, and roses came into view. The Tea Garden, nestled as it was in the concave disk below the hill where the hotel stood, would be the last to throw aside its misty blanket.

An outline of the fountain became visible, and shafts of sunlight cut through the outlying trees and burned at the fog, trying to reflect itself off the basin of water. Jeff wondered what else the water was reflecting. It had a red tinge to it, as if it were mimicking the hotel's trademark geraniums that bloomed on everything from the carpeting to the stationery.

The misty veil lifted. Jeff saw something — a tarp? — draped over the low stone wall of the pool that surrounded the fountain. His first thought was of the kid who'd been reamed out the night before for leaving the hedge clippers out. He was really in for it when his superior discovered the tarp in the fountain.

The sun broke full then, sharpening everything in the garden as if a spotlight had been turned onto the scene.

Jeff's grip went slack. He set down the cup of coffee to avoid dropping it. The tarp crumpled over the ledge wasn't a tarp but a jacket. Two arms extended from its sleeves at unnatural angles. The red wasn't a reflection; it was blood.

Jeff stumbled back into his room and dialed 911. Waiting, his heart thudding, he wondered whether the secluded island actually *had* 911. Then a dispatcher answered, and Jeff explained what he had seen. The woman assured him that she would send an ambulance, as well as the local police, to the hotel. Jeff hung up and flew out of the room.

Sirens whined in the distance as he reached the fountain. The slender body was dressed in a sport coat, jeans, and loafers without socks. Jeff spread his stance for support on the slick surface and propped one foot against the base of the fountain for leverage. He hooked his arms under those of the man and tried to lift.

The odd angle at which he had to stand, combined with the heavy, water-soaked clothing was more than Jeff expected. He strained against the efforts of the water, which seemed determined not to release its catch. Suddenly, with a loud sucking sound, body and water separated, and Jeff pulled the person over the fountain's wall.

Loafers without socks. He wondered why that was important.

There is an ominous, pounding silence during the seconds before a bell sounds. When a competition is about to start or your race against the clock is almost over and the anticipation builds within that silence and the pressure threatens to burst your eardrums and pound your heart through your chest.

That silence deafened Jeff as he turned the man over.

He met the cold, dead stare of Frank Hamilton.

Chapter Eleven

A makeshift interrogation room had been set up in a small office inside the hotel. It contained only a plain library table, which served as a desk, two chairs — one on either side — and a smaller table against the back wall. On the small table was a coffeepot and several cups, pitchers of ice water and glasses, and a silver tray piled high with doughnuts.

Jeff wondered absently how long the doughnuts would last after the cops showed.

It had been an hour since he'd found the body and, to his thinking, the investigation was getting off to a slow start.

At length, a lean man with salt-and-pepper hair — pepper was losing — and a mustache that had already given up the fight walked in and scanned the room. "Doughnuts," he said sarcastically. "What a friggin' surprise." He flung a manila folder onto the desk's surface as if he were skipping a stone across a pond, poured himself a cup of coffee, and removed his sport coat. He hung it on the chair and dropped into the seat. He identified himself as Detective Cal Brookner, pulled three pages from the folder, lined them up side by side.

After studying the sheets for a moment, he looked up. "FBI, huh?"

Jeff was surprised that this news had been uncovered so quickly, especially by such a small police department, and he said so.

"I was with Detroit PD for eighteen years," Brookner explained as he pulled a pack of cigarettes from his pocket and fished a book of matches out of the cellophane jacket. "Left in ninety-four to get away from death by unnatural causes, but I've kept my connections intact."

"Are you telling me that people don't have accidents in paradise?"

"In Paradise and Hell and every place in between." He saw the confused look on Jeff's face and said, "Names of Michigan towns. Inside joke." He set the cigarette on fire, blew out the match's flame, then looked for an ashtray. None was on the desk, so he used a saucer.

"Accidents, sure," the detective continued. "But this wasn't an accident." His voice seemed calmer now, and Jeff figured nicotine was to Brookner what caffeine was to him.

Jeff swigged more coffee. "I didn't think so. Quite a trick, if it were — fall forward and crack open the back of your head."

"Exactly. What did you do for the FBI?"

"A paper pusher, mostly. A hundred years ago. But you probably know that already."

"Something to do with antiques, this says."

"I investigated museum thefts, that sort of thing. Now I lead a calmer life. I look for antiques that people are willing to pay for."

"You're from Seattle. The victim was from Seattle." Brookner looked up. "Did you know him?"

"We ran into each other now and then, being in the same line of work."

"You know a lot about antiques?"

Jeff hesitated. "Goya scribbled *'Aun aprendo'* across one of the last sketches he did before he died. Means 'I am still learning.' That's me. I know quite a bit, but I've still got a long way to go. What I don't know, I research, or I ask people who do know. Plus, antiques are popular now, which means books about them are, too."

"My mother-in-law has cookie jars." Brookner's lips tightened. "You'd think she owned the New York Yankees."

Jeff leaned forward. "Are they Shawnee?"

"I think that's what she calls it. I thought she was talking about some kind of Indian pottery till she showed me the stuff. Looks like a bunch of pigs and puppies that some-body played dress-up with, if you ask me. Why?"

"Usually a good market for it. By the way, the name *did* come from the Shawnee Indians. One of their arrowheads was found on the land where the plant was to be built. The company operated for only about twenty years, so that's a key factor in collecting the stuff. The factory shut down when it couldn't compete with foreign imports after World War II. Another factor: They used paper labels for identification, and those didn't last if the kitchenware was actually used. So, pieces in good condition with the labels intact bring top dollar." Jeff stopped and took a deep breath. "Sorry, Detective. I didn't mean to stray from your investigation. But, depending on what pieces your mother-in-law has, those cookie jars could be worth thousands."

"No shit?" Brookner let out a low whistle.

"Hard to believe, for noncollectors."

"You've taken all the fun out of giving her hell, Talbot." Brookner checked another sheet. "Did Frank Hamilton collect antiques?"

Jeff had never thought about Hamilton's personal life. "I don't know, to tell you the truth."

"Was he an expert in any particular field?"

"Possibly."

"Didn't keep up with the competition very well, did you?"

"Only when it counted. Sure, Hamilton and I ran into each other from time to time. Hell, we even bought from each other on occasion. But I spend a lot more time studying antiques than I do pickers."

Someone rapped the doorjamb.

A woman in a navy blue uniform stood there, holding a bicycle helmet. Her name-plate read Littlefield. She was American Indian (Jeff wondered if Brookner had ever asked *her* about Shawnee ware), short and stocky, with smooth brown skin, high cheekbones, and that proud, defiant look in her eyes that put Jeff in mind of Geronimo. Normally, he could pinpoint someone's age, but this one had him stumped. She could've been anywhere between twenty-five and forty.

"What've you got, Mel?" Brookner said.

"They finally finished draining the fountain. Found this lug wrench at the bottom." She put a large bag containing an L-shaped length of metal on the desk. "I have to wonder what it's doing on the island. Ironic, isn't it, to get killed with a lug wrench on an island without cars? Except for the emergency vehicles, of course." The woman spoke with an odd combination of pinched and singsong syllables.

Brookner started to say something, but she cut him off.

"Been there, done that. Our Explorer and the ambulance share the same garage. No tools missing."

"Mel, this is Jeff Talbot. FBI. Was, anyway. He's some sort of antiques expert now. He found the body."

"Yeah? You ever been on that tee-vee show?"

"What?"

"That tee-vee show. People bringing in antiques for the experts to tell them that Aunt Millie's butt-ugly vase is worth ten thousand bucks. My sister watches it." Littlefield handed Brookner a slip of paper.

Brookner handed her a question. "Cookout still on for tonight?"

Mel chuckled. "Do I look like I'm gonna cancel a cookout just because someone got clocked on the island?" She was gone before the detective could respond.

"Interesting accent for a Native American," Jeff said.

"What? Oh, Littlefield. Yeah, I've gotten used to that Yooper accent. You know Yooper?"

Jeff shook his head.

"Upper Peninsula. U.P. Yooper. It's a carry-over from Scandinavian settlers." Brookner read the paper left by Littlefield. "Hamilton left an emergency number with the hotel when he checked in. Seattle exchange. No answer, though. And it's — what? — two, three hours earlier there?"

"Three."

"Uh-huh." The detective stared at Jeff. "Know anyone who'd want to kill him?"

"No. But like I said, I didn't know too much about him." Jeff realized that he knew Hamilton's business approach but virtually nothing about his personal life.

Brookner watched him another minute,

then said, "The medical examiner ferried over with me. She'll work fast. Got a Lions game she wants to watch this afternoon. Says she'll kill the guy all over again if he makes her miss it.

"One more question," Brookner continued. "Did you know Hamilton was here?"

"No. Yes. I mean, I didn't know he was *coming* here. But I saw him last night, from up in the bar —"

"The one up top?"

Jeff nodded. "The Cupola. Hell of a view from up there. I looked down, saw him in the gardens talking to someone."

Brookner's brows raised. It was his turn to lean forward.

"Sorry, Detective. I can't identify her —"

"Her?"

"Yes, her. At least, I hope it was a woman. She had on a picture hat. You know, big brim. Dark dress, too. Probably black. It was hard to tell."

"*Breakfast at Tiffany's?*"

"That's what it reminded me of," Jeff said. An immediate image of Jennifer Hurst popped into his brain. He wondered if he should tell the detective that he'd just described what Jennifer was wearing the night before. The night Frank Hamilton was killed. He decided to sit on it since she wasn't the only one whose clothes fit the description. "I don't envy you your job, Detective. There were probably twenty women dressed like that last night."

Brookner shook his head wearily. "You'll be here tonight, won't you?"

Jeff said he would.

"If we don't come up with anything by then, we may have to put a couple officers down there with a radio, see if re-creating it sheds any light. You can show me from up top where Hamilton and his lady friend were standing."

"I don't know that I'd call her his friend. Looked like they were arguing."

"Arguing?" Brookner's eyes narrowed. "And how the hell do you know they were arguing?"

"Body language. I could tell something was going on."

"Yeah? And did you know it was Hamilton?"

"I didn't at first. But that boiled down to body language, too. You see, Hamilton has this habit when he's angry. He pops his forehead, like this." Jeff demonstrated. "Only with his left hand instead of his right."

"So, you've seen him angry?"

Jeff's lips tightened. He hadn't seen that one coming. Maybe he had been out of investigating for too long. "It might help if you know Hamilton's work ethics. He's like a hungry car salesman. If his tactics don't work, he pushes pretty hard. I saw him

Thursday. An old woman had to threaten to call the cops on him if he didn't leave her property."

"You know the old woman?"

"No." Jeff told the detective about checking out the sale early. "I wrote her a check, but she told me her name was hard to spell and that she'd fill it in herself. It'll be hard to track since today's Saturday." Jeff took a drink and winced. Nothing worse than cold coffee. "Wait a minute. She was having a two-day estate sale. If you want to make sure she's still in Washington, have the authorities check. I jotted her address in my notebook from the ad in the paper. It's in my room."

Brookner told Jeff to get the notebook. "And, Talbot, you know the drill, so don't make me say it."

"Don't leave town."

"Right." Brookner left. Once outside, he yelled, "Somebody get those damn doughnuts out of there."

Chapter Twelve

After copying the estate sale information from his notebook, Jeff found Officer Mel Littlefield, gave her the slip of paper, then checked his watch. It was 8:30, so he made his way to the dining room for breakfast.

The huge room was animated, filled with the metallic tinkle of silver against china, the clatter of cup against saucer, the chatter of people making plans for the day. Many didn't even seem to be aware of what they were eating, so intent were they upon finishing so they could move on. Jeff refused to sit down to a meal with that agenda. Sheila had instilled in him the desire to savor a meal for its own merits, not rush through it without an appreciative and conscious nod to the chef who had created it.

The dining room was busy, and Jeff stood just inside the entrance, scanning the room and waiting for the return of the maître d', when Ben caught his eye and motioned him over to the table where he was sitting. Jennifer was there, too, along with Edward Davenport.

As Jeff walked toward the trio, he picked

up pieces of conversation about the body that had been found earlier on the premises. Speculation, mostly. Observation. Some were complaining about their newfound knowledge that there were motorized vehicles on the island, saying it ruined the ambience, while others voiced relief that emergency services were available. They touted that one never knew when one might need an ambulance.

Jennifer laughed in response to something Davenport was saying. The auctioneer was rather jovial, quite different from the night before. Jeff figured him to be a morning person. He would be, too, just as soon as he'd had another pot of coffee.

"Good morning," Jeff said. "Everyone here seems to be in high spirits." He accepted the waiter's offer of coffee, grateful that he'd come around so quickly, then ordered a fritatta and orange juice.

"Aren't you?" Jennifer passed him a basket of assorted pastries. "It's going to be a perfect day. Lots of sun, lots of antiques."

"If I can get that sort of day jump-started, sure. I've spent the last couple hours with detectives and dead men."

"You're kidding," Ben said. "Why?"

"That's how an investigation tends to go when you're the one who finds the body."

Jennifer almost choked on her orange juice. "*You* found him?"

"I'm afraid so. And, as it turns out, I know

him — rather, I know who he is. Was. God, I'll never get used to that. He's from Seattle."

Ben spoke up. "So you know who it was. We've been trying to find out, but no one will give us a straight answer."

"Maybe you knew him, although I'm not sure whether he'd attended this festival before. His name was Frank Hamilton."

Jeff watched his companions as he spoke, but all three had bowed their heads slightly, as if concentrating, trying to find the name in their memory banks. Jeff thought how difficult it was to read someone when you couldn't look into their eyes.

One by one, the three stated that they didn't know the man.

Ben added, "I might know him if I saw him. But we talk to so many people at these things. . . . The name doesn't ring any bells."

"You said you knew him. What kind of person was he?" asked Jennifer.

"Well, he wasn't easy to get along with, but that could describe a lot of people. It's not a motive for murder, though."

It was Davenport's turn to choke. He set his cup down hard, splashing coffee onto the white linen tablecloth. "Murder? I heard he slipped on the wet grass and split his head on the ledge of the fountain."

"He slipped, all right. But it looks like he had some help from behind."

Davenport's happy mood faded. "The next thing the bobbies will want is alibis. And the only way I could have an alibi for the night is if I had employed the company of a woman — which I most certainly did not." He eyed Jeff. "You're here alone, too, aren't you, Talbot?"

"Afraid so. It's not always wise to be alone in one's room, is it?"

"At least we've got that covered," Ben announced with a smile and no small amount of relief in his tone.

"That's right," Jennifer responded. "It helps to be inseparable, doesn't it?" She leaned over and lightly kissed her husband's cheek.

"Except around midnight," Jeff said.

The couple's eyes widened.

"Are you telling us that *you* were with Jennifer last night?" Davenport winked, obviously trying to lighten the mood again.

Jeff ignored him and addressed Jennifer. "You left the bar before Ben, remember? You were going to make a stop in the ladies' room, then meet Ben in your room."

"Well, yes. But it was only for something like three minutes. Who on earth could have gotten from the Cupola Bar to the Tea Garden that quickly? Not to mention have some sort of confrontation with someone you know — I *assume* the victim knew the killer, since the police said the man's wallet was still on him."

"Who told you about the wallet? The police?"

"No, but I heard one of the other guests mention it earlier. Everyone's talking about it, you know. At any rate, Ben says they'll have to interview all the guests. He and I were together all evening. I don't see what difference two or three minutes can make."

Jeff listened for any sign of nervousness while Jennifer spoke, but found none.

"Ben?" Jeff prompted, surprised that the young man hadn't offered any sort of explanation.

Ben shrugged his shoulders. "She's right. We met back in the room. Matter of fact, she told me that she'd gone straight to the room. 'Why stop at a ladies' room, when our own room was so close?' That's what she said."

"Ben, I feel like we're being questioned now, don't you?" Jennifer pushed chunks of melon around on her plate. "Jeff, are you working as an undercover cop or something?"

"I'm sorry." Jeff didn't want to have to explain his background unless he had to. "It's just my curious nature, I guess. I like trying to fit puzzle pieces together."

Davenport cleared his throat. "Well. I say we try and put this behind us. There is much to be done, and I think it would be better if we continued with our schedules until the police decide who they will — and won't — be interrogating." He checked his watch, gave the face a quick tap. "Ah, my seminar begins in ten. Will you all be attending?"

"Wouldn't miss it," Ben said with a smile.

"Very well then." Davenport stood. "I'll see you there."

Jeff watched as the tall auctioneer hurried toward the exit.

Jennifer dabbed at the corners of her mouth, then stood and placed the napkin in her chair. "Ben, I'm going to powder my nose and pick up a pad and paper before Edward's session." She turned to Jeff. "Unless you think I shouldn't go anywhere alone. Do my husband and I need to be joined at the hip?" She left without waiting for an answer.

Ben shook his head. "I'm sorry, Jeff. Jennifer goes on the defensive pretty quickly. Comes from having overprotective parents. I stopped trying to figure her out a long time ago. But, hell, there's no need for her to get upset. We didn't even know the guy."

"No need to apologize."

Ben stood. "I'd better be in the Terrace Room when she gets there. Are you coming?"

"Go ahead. I'll be there in a few minutes."

After Ben left, Jeff accepted a coffee refill and thought about his conversation with Ben the night before. How long had they talked after Jennifer left the Cupola Bar? He and Ben had gotten caught up in reminiscing about their best antique finds. Both agreed:

A best find didn't necessarily have to be the most valuable one, monetarily speaking.

After Ben had mentioned his sports memorabilia, he'd talked about his gun collection and how he'd tracked down a musket that had belonged to one of his ancestors who'd fought in the American Revolution. Jeff had been so fascinated by the account, he had no way of pinpointing how long they'd talked before Ben had suddenly said that Jennifer would be out looking for him if he didn't get to their room.

The whole thing bothered him, but he wasn't sure why. If the Hursts had known Hamilton, it would've been different. Still, Jennifer Hurst didn't have an alibi. Not only had Jeff seen her in a large hat and black dress similar to those worn by the woman in the garden, but also she had several minutes unaccounted for.

Right now, that was the least of Jeff's worries. He wasn't fooled by Detective Brookner's friendly attitude toward him. Some detectives came on like avenging angels, others plied you with fellowship and good humor while they secretly spun a web around you. Jeff was no unsuspecting fly. Until a better suspect surfaced, he knew that Brookner's list had only one name: Jeffrey Talbot.

Chapter Thirteen

The Terrace Room was decorated in an Asian theme, with jade-colored wallpaper featuring an urn design in salmon above a dado of Chinese lattice. If you missed the Oriental effect, you were probably too busy staring at the beasts that dominated the room.

They flanked the stage: two enormous, bronzed fu dogs on platforms the size of bankers' desks. Both the male, with his meaty paw on the world, and the female, protecting her young, snarled viciously as if to say that anyone taking the stage would be guarded against interlopers.

Jeff pulled his attention from them and looked around. Although he'd been here the night before, he had only poked his head in. Now he realized that he'd missed the chinoiserie entirely.

The atmosphere today was completely different from last night. People who had danced and laughed now sat quietly in chairs lined up in long rows to create an auditorium setting. Although the stage was still equipped with a grand piano, trap set, and speakers, the instruments seemed naked and out of place without their musicians. A podium had been placed at the front of the stage. Behind the podium and off to its left, Edward Davenport sat quietly going over something written on a notepad. A hotel employee was busy raising the microphone, having obviously noted the speaker's immense height.

The room was packed. Jeff finally located a vacant seat in the back and slid into the chair while the auctioneer was being introduced. According to the program, the session would last until ten-thirty.

Edward Davenport took his place behind the podium and waited for the applause to subside. After making a few opening remarks, he paused. The sound of papers rustling died down. Someone coughed. A throat cleared. Finally, all noise stopped, and every eye in the room was on the auctioneer. Only then did he resume.

"Journey with me to another place and time. You are in the throes of a war-torn England . . ."

Jeff couldn't tell whether the auctioneer was really this passionate about his subject or if, perhaps, he relied on theatrics as a way of capturing his audience. Either way, it had its effect.

Jeff remembered reading somewhere that English history was one of Davenport's areas of expertise. At least that meant the information should be reliable.

". . . and today," the auctioneer was saying, "The War of the Roses seems an odd name for a war. We look upon roses as a thing of beauty, do we not? But remember: War disguised in beauty is still war. There are others: the War of the Austrian Succession, the Seven Years' War, the Battle of Waterloo.

"Yes, Waterloo was Great Britain's victory. People tend to get so caught up in the fact that it was Napoleon's undoing, they forget what it did for our beloved England. Until Waterloo, Napoleon's control had vastly crippled British trade. What does that have to do with us now? We'll get to that in a moment.

"First, though, let's visit one of the wars." Davenport paused, leaned into the microphone. "Listen," he implored. "Hear it? Gunfire cracking, bombs exploding. Feel the ground quake as cannons buck, belching hot orbs of destruction all around you." He grew louder with each word, his voice shaking the room.

"Join me. Close your eyes," Davenport beseeched. "Envision with me the buildings. Look at the destruction, the bombing, the burning. Do you see it? Do you *see* what we lost?"

Jeff looked around him. It was a large crowd, and virtually everyone was following Davenport's instruction. Eyes closed, they were under his charismatic spell. Many were leaning forward in their seats, drawn into the fold by the speaker's mesmerizing voice. It was like a tent revival, Jeff thought. Davenport was an evangelist, preaching fire and brimstone.

Jeff's lack of sleep caught up to him. He closed his eyes. The events of the morning played before him as if a projector's switch had been flicked on. And while Davenport spoke of destruction, Jeff saw it on its most human level.

He's trying to thread his hands under the arms of the dead weight, trying to balance himself, hefting the man, hoping he's strong enough to clear the stone wall, turning the man carefully onto his back. He shifts a hand to the back of the man's head, cradles it, lowers it gently to the stone walkway surrounding the fountain. The face is swollen, its flesh translucent gray, its lips a dark purple blue, its eyes void of emotion, void of anything. Jeff's gaze is transfixed upon a jagged gash, and he follows it from above the left eye and down along the temple. The base of the skull feels spongy, the bones shift unnaturally in his palm. This doesn't completely register, and he doesn't jerk his hand away. He scans the form, sees the jacket, the jeans, the shoes without socks. His eyes widen with realization. His gaze darts back to the bloated face. His suspicions are confirmed. It is Frank Hamilton.

Something banged. Jeff jumped. Davenport had slammed his fist against the podium.

"Imagine the effect," the auctioneer was saying, "that those wars had on the English antiques we prize today."

Beads of perspiration popped on Jeff's forehead.

Davenport smiled sadly. "Now you understand, don't you? Without the depredations of war, without the destruction, the fires, the vandalism — without all that, those material things that survived wouldn't have the value we now place upon them . . ."

Jeff willed himself to stay in the present. He had to admit it: Davenport's angle was fascinating. Not many people thought about the material things lost in the path of war. Billions of dollars' worth — perhaps more — of furniture, glassware, silver, gold, textiles, documents were purged from existence during those devastating times in history. Really, could a price be attached? The remaining items, those that survived the holocausts, were far more valuable, both in sentiment and in dollars.

"Yes," Davenport was saying. "I can see that you share in my anguish. Only God knows how much we lost. *But* . . ." Davenport paused. The audience held its collective breath. "But," he repeated, this time with less emphasis, "look what we have gained. In addition to our freedom, of course. We have gained an inordinate respect for those things that survived. A reverence, if you will, for the hand-carved oak table that did not burn, for the encrusted sterling silver with its royal hallmarks that did not melt, for the forged weapons that survived at the hands of maniacs, for the very documents that speak of freedom, of heritage."

Despite Davenport's evangelical magnetism, Jeff had trouble focusing on the speech. He couldn't seem to get the vision of Hamilton out of his mind. As if to erase the nightmare, he rubbed his eyes. Like a charge of electricity, a lightning-quick current transmitted him back to the scene.

He turns from the face, sees two patches of earth between the walkway's stones, patches rubbed bare where once there was grass. He frowns, examines the toes of the brown loafers. Snagged between sole and soft leather are spiky green blades, imbedded in packed mud. He shivers, realizing that Hamilton didn't die instantly.

He hears sirens, looks up and sees paramedics loping across the lawn. Others, too, are streaming down the hill toward him. Toward the fountain. Toward death.

Jeff shuddered, drawing the attention of an old man seated next to him.

The man poked Jeff in the ribs and grinned. "Did you fall asleep in church, young fella?"

Jeff apologized, dragged himself back once again, to the present. The eloquent auctioneer had begun taking questions from a captive and participatory audience.

After several well-received responses, Davenport started to dismiss the large crowd. Someone spoke up from the back of the room. Jeff recognized the voice.

"I have a question, Mr. Davenport." It was Detective Cal Brookner. "Did you know Frank Hamilton?"

Fu dogs aren't all they're cracked up to be, Jeff thought.

Chapter Fourteen

Without waiting for an answer from Davenport, Detective Brookner told everyone to sit back down. He walked to the podium, pulled the mike down a good eight inches, and cut to the chase. "Most of you know by now that there's been a murder." A smattering of gasps came from those in the audience who'd had their heads buried in the sand all morning. "We'll need to talk with several of you. It should go without saying, but I'll say it anyway so there will be no confusion: *No one* is to leave the island. It's going to take a lot of manpower, but we *will* have people screening everyone at the ferry landings. If you're registered at this hotel, then you won't be leaving until we've had a chance to talk with you and given the okay. Understand?" Obviously, the question wasn't meant to elicit an answer. He turned to Davenport. "You come with me." The auctioneer followed the detective out of the room.

"Why, how rude."

Jeff turned and saw that the remark had come from Ruth Ann Longan, one of the three Southern women he'd met the night before. She was seated down the row from him, along with Asia Graham. Today, Asia was wearing a bright red pantsuit. To Jeff, the penguin effect from the night before remained intact, making her look today like a penguin in a red pantsuit. He approached them. "Good morning, ladies."

"Mr. Talbot, don't you agree?" Ruth Ann's voice was high-pitched.

"The police have to do their job, and it's not an easy one in this case."

"Well, yes, of course. But Mr. Davenport did such a fine job, and to have his grand finale diluted like that just doesn't seem right."

"Ruthie, honey." Asia used her cane for counterbalance and struggled to her feet as she spoke. The effort put extra emphasis in her voice. "The sooner they do their job, the sooner things around here will get back to normal."

"She's right," Jeff said.

"I'm sure she is," Ruth Ann conceded. "Asia? Didn't you buy something last year from that young man who was killed this morning? I seem to recall —"

"You know, you're right. I'd forgotten all about that." Asia addressed Jeff. "He showed up here at the festival with a slave document. Gave me a pretty fair price for it, too. I was leery, at first. But then he pointed out that he'd spoken with me — with all of us — the year before. I was astounded when he rattled off what each and every one of us collect."

"That's impressive all right." Jeff looked beyond Asia. "Someone's missing from your group. Lily?"

"Lily's missing?" Ruth Ann turned and looked, then said, "Oh, I remember. She was positively craving some fudge. We sent her downtown, for fear she might have an attack of the vapors. We told her that we would report anything of interest from the seminar."

Asia began moving to the end of the row. "Looks like we'll have plenty to report, doesn't it, Mr. Talbot?"

"I wish you ladies would call me Jeff. Does Lily have a favorite fudge shop on the island?" He made a mental note to pick up the fudge he'd promised Sheila.

"Oh, that woman thinks she's a connoisseur." Ruth Ann emphasized *connoisseur.* "She buys from several, then holds her own taste test."

"That sounds tempting, but I have to get some work done first." Jeff excused himself and set out to find the Brighton Pavilion. The items that would be auctioned on Sunday were displayed there, and he was anxious to get his first look at the cabaret set. He'd been told the room would be open between the scheduled lectures.

Several others were already there when he arrived, but the room was locked. An employee made his way through the crowd and taped a makeshift sign to the door that read Closed, after which a woman announced loudly, "we already knew that." The employee shrugged, then left without comment. The crowd dispersed.

Needing a diversion, Jeff spent the next hour or so perusing the booths in the other conference rooms.

One vendor offered several inkwells. Fortunately, Jeff had begun carrying a list of what Sheila had so as to avoid duplication, and he always checked it before purchasing. Of course, his wife still had several packages in her "store," but he knew that if they ended up with a duplicate, he could always sell it to Blanche or one of his other clients.

He purchased two travelers, inkwells designed for journeys before the inventions of the reservoir and fountain pens in the late 1800s. Both of Jeff's purchases were leather, and their lids were spring-loaded with thumb release buttons. Beyond that, each had its own distinct personality. One was English and reminded him of a butler: tall and resolute and dressed in black. Its sterling silver top was polished to a warm glow, and its edge was hand engraved in an elaborate floral design in a circle that formed a cartouche. The center of the cartouche was monogrammed with the initials DRB in an elegant script, and the underside of the lid was hallmarked Birmingham 1888. The box contained a flawless crystal insert in which to transfer ink.

The French traveler was like a rich Parisian woman, wrapped in brown crocodile with a body shaped long and low as if reclining on a chaise longue. The interior was chased gold, with compartments holding a matching gold-plated inkwell, roller blotter, and a cylinder for storing nibs.

Normally, Jeff wouldn't pay the several hundred dollars that the vendor was asking for the two, but travelers weren't as easy to come by as desk inkwells. It made sense that they would cost more and besides, he wanted to return home with more for Sheila than a box of fudge.

It seemed odd to him, purchasing something called a traveler for a woman who may never again travel. Then he realized he collected snuff boxes, but he didn't dip snuff. He sure as hell wasn't going to start, either. What did it matter? he asked himself. When you collect, there doesn't have to be a criterion. Only a passion.

He purchased two circa 1835 lithographs featuring birds for a client who was redecorating her office in Seattle's Pioneer Building. She was an avid collector of antique bird prints, and Jeff knew she wouldn't even flinch at the mid-five-figure price tag. The lithographs were hand-colored by John and Elizabeth Gould (John Gould was also the lithographer), and each print showcased two birds with black, red, and yellow coloring.

Jeff purchased a few other items, arranged to have everything but the inkwells shipped back to Seattle, and returned to the Brighton Pavilion on the off chance that it was open.

He was in luck. A young man in a burgundy blazer (hotel security, Jeff guessed) was unlocking the door while a small man with a head of thick, snowy white hair looked on. Apparently hearing the rustle of Jeff's shopping bag, they turned. The old man smiled, and his bushy brows raised inquiringly.

Jeff guessed him to be in his early seventies. His eyes were a cloudy gray and held none of the sentiment of the smile. Blue veins showed on hands with nails in need of clipping. The nails were clean, though, white with bright pink beds as though they'd been recently scrubbed. The man nodded and gestured with one hand, a get-on-with-it orchestration that told Jeff to state his purpose.

"I'm here to take a look at one of the items?" Jeff posed his statement in the form of a question, hoping to lead the old man into another nod. He would take it as an affirmative.

"Mr. Davenport was to be in charge of this," the man said, "but I've been told he is with the police."

What Jeff had originally taken as a smile

was apparently a set of ill-fitting dentures that prevented the old man's mouth from shutting completely.

"I doubt the police still have him," Jeff said.

"I wouldn't know about that. I was told that the room will remain closed to the general public until word is received from Mr. Davenport."

"When I had breakfast with him this morning, he said there would be no problem with my coming by to view one of the auction items. Do you work for him?"

"No, I do not work for him. Now, if you will excuse me." The old man turned to the security guard, who pushed open the door and gave Jeff a warning look.

Jeff addressed the old man. "May I join you, sir?" He realized he was beginning to sound desperate. He'd waited for years to see the cabaret set. Suddenly, he could wait no longer. "I assure you I won't take much of your time."

"I'm afraid not. No one is allowed in until Mr. Davenport arrives."

Jeff needed a different approach. "Please." If he hadn't sounded desperate before, he did now. That was not his intent, and begging wasn't his idea of a different approach. "Just a look at Josephine's cabaret set. Please."

"Josephine's?" The old man smiled now, and Jeff saw a noticeable difference from before. "You speak her name as if you know her intimately. Rather, knew her. She's dead, you know. Are you Napoleon reincarnated?"

Jeff returned the smile. He wasn't sure why he had called it Josephine's. Perhaps it was because he'd been reading the letter of provenance so much lately. Josephine's signature intrigued him. The small script was more in keeping with a teenage girl, not an empress. Its closely looped letters and lower case *j* possessed an unexpected playful quality. Her *e*s spoke volumes, always leaning back toward the direction from which they'd come. "I . . ." He shrugged, unsure of how to explain himself.

The letter of provenance. He withdrew his copy, along with the photo of the tea set, from his wallet and handed them to the man.

The man carefully unfolded the letter. After reading it, he refolded it and handed it back. Jeff grinned sheepishly. "I've been looking for the set for many years."

The man studied the photograph. At length, he looked up. The gray eyes misted. "My wife's name is Josephine. We own the set. Come with me."

Reverently, Jeff stepped inside. He'd anticipated this moment for so long and now skepticism crept over him. He wondered if he'd be disappointed when he saw the cabaret set. Then he realized that his feelings didn't matter. Blanche's did, however, and he hoped she wouldn't be disappointed. Things from one's childhood rarely held up under the scrutinizing and practical eye of an adult.

"Name's Curtis Pettigrew," the man said as he flipped on a light switch. "I suppose I should know yours."

"You're right, sir. Of course. I'm Jeff Talbot."

The security guard bolted the door and stationed himself in front of it.

The room was deafeningly silent yet charged with an energy that one could only describe as the pulse of history.

Jeff would fully realize this later, when he remembered that the room was filled with a fortune in antiques. But for now he was only aware that it held the one treasure he was seeking.

It was the same sensation he'd had in antique shops when he'd spied something he'd been searching for, something he'd thought would never surface. He couldn't bring himself to approach it. Not yet. He'd hold his breath. *Don't get too excited. It may not be what you think it is, what you're praying it is.*

Now, he reminded himself to breathe, to put one foot in front of the other and follow the old man.

The set was in a glass display case the size and shape of a casket, arranged as if it might be pressed into service at any moment for high tea. Placed to the side was the Moroccan case (large enough to have elicited questioning stares from airport employees who monitor carry-on baggage dimensions), which had housed and protected the rare pieces for over two hundred years.

Jeff's gaze darted quickly between the tea set and the leather case, checking that each piece had its own resting place. Each did. The set was complete: The large pot, the sugar bowl and creamer, the two cup and saucer sets, and the massive tray upon which it all now stood.

The elaborate gilding that ran along the borders of the fitted case matched the Napoleonic bees that were stitched in gold upon the ivory silk lining.

The finials on the lids of the teapot and sugar bowl were also gold bees, with eyes of cabochon rubies and bodies of remarkable detail.

And Josephine's beloved swans were everywhere. The handles were golden, every one a slender neck that led down to a body whose flared wings gripped the bowl. One could almost hear their cries as they clung to such beauty. Rich claret served as a ground for cartouches upon which water scenes were painted and elaborately framed with swirls of gold. Swans glided through the paintings as well, each scene varying slightly but all incorporating the poetic fowl and pink-cheeked maidens and pastoral surroundings. The artist's hand had been exacting, and one could see the motion of the water, the sway of the branches as the scenes unfolded.

Jeff saw that someone's hands were on the case's glass, their palms flat against it as if feeling for a pulse. He stepped back, realizing they were his. He didn't remember dropping his shopping bag, or reaching out, or even how he'd gotten to where he was.

Obviously sensing Jeff's enchantment, Pettigrew unlocked the case and carefully withdrew one of the cups. If it weren't for the long nails, the man might easily have dropped the irreplaceable item. Jeff wondered then if he grew them for this specific purpose. It seemed right, practical.

Transfixed, Jeff held out cupped hands.

"Sit down first," Pettigrew admonished, as if he were about to place a newborn baby into the arms of an excitable six-year-old.

Jeff sat.

The delicate cup felt warm in his hands, and he wondered if it did have a soul after all. Then he realized that his hands were cold, clammy. This reaction surprised him. He'd been moved by antiques before, but nothing had affected him like this. His heart pounded. He was holding the cup that Josephine had held two *centuries* before him.

He wanted to turn it over, look at the maker's mark that would be a milky blue

136

underglaze. He wanted to see the Republic mark that had replaced the Louis XV and Louis XVI cursive double *L*s.

But he couldn't move.

Chapter Fifteen

Sensory overload. He'd heard others talk about it, try to put it in terms that one who had never experienced it might understand. *Impossible,* he now realized, unless you've been there.

Jeff had no other explanation for his actions. He was in his room and had only a vague recollection of Curtis Pettigrew taking the cup and returning it to the display. Jeff couldn't remember whether he'd thanked the old man.

He needed to get away from the festival for awhile, away from the hotel. After locking the inkwells in his suite's safe, he put on the vest Sheila had given him and outfitted it with what he thought he might need. Downstairs, he acquired a map from the concierge and set out to explore the island.

When he stepped outside, Jeff felt as if he'd spent the last few hours underground. The events of the morning — from Hamilton's death to Davenport's session to Jeff's own cocooning among the antiques to the cabaret — had been so surreal that now the bright sunlight seemed harsh, invading.

As he started down the long, curved sidewalk that bordered the hill above the Tea Garden, he paused and studied the fountain. It looked strange, lifeless without the shell-shaped fountains around its perimeter spewing little waterfalls into the large basin.

He checked his watch. It was almost noon. He couldn't believe that only this morning he'd found Hamilton's body down there.

At the bottom of the hill he consulted the map, then turned right and strolled along the boardwalk, following the wide loop toward the docks and the central shopping area of the island.

Main Street was crowded as a constant stream of people poured through the shop-lined breezeways that led from the docks.

The concierge had told Jeff that the Tea Room at Fort Mackinac served a great lunch with a view of the Straits. It sounded like a strange combination, but Jeff welcomed the opportunity to squeeze in a visit to the fort. Military history had always fascinated him. He saw it, perched high on a hill overlooking Lake Huron and recognized its great vantage point so important back when the British protected the island from French invasion. Tables with bright yellow umbrellas were lined up in a row along the ledge like canaries perched on a wire.

Jeff struggled to climb the steep hill, noting several times that he needed to use the workout room at home more often. He half expected the island's year-round residents to be in fantastic shape but, more often than not, the theory didn't prove out. Obviously, though, they'd built incredible stamina. By the time he reached the fort, he decided that stamina beat muscle all to hell.

He lingered over lunch in order to catch his breath and contemplated whether or not to take the time required for touring the fort. Getting there had taken longer than he'd anticipated, and he recognized his own criteria for such a large chunk of history. Rushing through the Revolution was not his idea of a tour.

He settled for a quick tour of the Sutler's Store, picking up a book on the fort's history for himself and a Michigan cookbook for Sheila.

Working his way back down the hill proved to be almost as challenging as the trip up had been, but he finally arrived on Main Street and fought his way through the crowds.

He was debating the practicality of getting some Mackinac Island fudge to Seattle intact when he looked up and thought he recognized a woman crossing the street at the end of the block.

He told himself that he was imagining things. Why would she be here? The bizarre events of the last few hours were taking their toll on his senses.

But he couldn't let it go. Juggling packages from the fort's gift shop and his Main Street purchases, he worked his way up the street, craning his neck in an attempt to keep the girl in sight. He caught a glimpse of her darting across the main thoroughfare, heading toward the fort. He cringed. If she went up there, she'd have to do it alone.

He picked up his pace, tried to catch her before she got that far. But he hadn't yet grown accustomed to the horse-drawn wagons. When one stopped in front of him, he geed instead of hawed and ended up having to circle around the back of the eight-bench cab. When he finally surfaced on the other side, the young woman had disappeared.

Damn it, he thought, the girl may as well have been driving a race car.

Chapter Sixteen

Blanche had said nothing about her assistant coming to Mackinac Island. Surely she knew Trudy Blessing was there, didn't she? There would be no reason for her *not* to know. But the bigger question was why. Why would Trudy be there, of all places?

Jeff frowned. It boiled down to one of two things: Coincidence or . . . or, what? A plot? A plot to spy on him? Why would anyone want to spy on him? He didn't have any secrets from Blanche. Well, except for the cabaret set. Was that it? Had Blanche gotten word about the cabaret set and decided to hedge her bet? Did she send Trudy, hoping that the wallflower would blend in? Was Trudy Blessing actually there to spy on him? He'd never before had reason to believe Blanche didn't trust him. Jeff cut it in every angle he could possibly think of. Nothing else came to him.

He knew one thing. All this speculation was fraying his nerves — nerves that were already frayed enough. He needed answers and, fortunately, this was one mystery he *could* solve.

He returned to his hotel.

She picked up on the fourth ring.

"Blanche, it's Jeff."

"Jeffrey? What on earth? You're the last person I expected to hear from."

"That's a two-way street."

"What? I didn't call you. What's going on?"

"That's what I want to know. Does her being here have something to do with me?"

"You're not making any sense. Her *who,* Jeff?"

"Trudy, that's who. Why is she here?"

"Trudy's where? In Michigan? You've got to be kidding me."

"Come on, Blanche. Don't tell me you didn't know."

"No, I didn't. Yesterday, Trudy asked for a few days' vacation. It was last minute but, quite frankly, I was thrilled that she'd actually asked. It's rare for her to do anything for herself, so I told her to take as much time as she wanted. Jeffrey, what's going on?"

"Blanche, are you telling me the truth? Or did you send her here to spy on me?"

"Jeffrey Talbot! Have you lost your senses? Why on *earth* would I need to spy on you?"

Blanche's tone and the use of Jeff's full name reminded him of his Auntie Pim when he'd done something wrong. Jeff's resolve crumbled. "Blanche, I'm sorry."

"You've been having to say that a lot lately. I've got a little saying for you: Throw dirt and you lose ground. Remember that next time you chew out an old lady."

He dropped onto the bed. "You're right. I know it's no excuse, but it's been a hell of a strange morning, and then seeing Trudy so far removed from Seattle threw me off my game." He let out his breath. "I can't make sense of any of it."

"You said 'strange morning.' Is there something stranger than seeing Trudy on the island?"

"You know Frank Hamilton?"

"Sure. He occasionally brings items into the shop. Has a good eye for antiques, but not much bedside manner. Don't tell me he's there, too? Good Lord, am I the only Seattleite still in Seattle?"

"There's one less here. I found Hamilton this morning. Dead."

"*Dead?*" She was quiet. Then: "How?"

"Don't know yet. By the looks of things, though, it wasn't an accident. After that, I decided to get away from the hotel for awhile, and then I saw Trudy. I wasn't sure what to think —"

"So you thought I'd sent her to spy on you. What are you up to that would cause me to spy on you? Selling my private wish list to the highest bidder?"

"Not a chance." Jeff relaxed a little. "May I

plead temporary insanity as far as this phone call is concerned?"

"You may." Blanche cleared her throat. "I'm with you, though. It's curious. Of course, I mentioned to Trudy that the island is magnificent. Maybe she's finally decided to come out of her shell and live a little."

"Well, I'm going to try and track her down. God knows how. It'll take me all day to call every hotel and bed-and-breakfast on this place."

There was a pause. "Jeff, wait. I may be able to help. The shop phoned me this morning and said that Trudy had called. She was worried that she'd forgotten and left the bank deposit sitting on my desk. Took me by surprise because she never forgets that sort of thing.

"The Saturday crew looked but, of course, they didn't find anything." Blanche was quiet again, obviously thinking. "Let me call the shop, have someone check the caller ID."

"Won't someone else have erased it by now?"

"Why would they? That's Trudy's job."

Jeff said good-bye and cradled the receiver gently. While he waited for Blanche to call back, he recapped the events thus far. It didn't take long. The big question was: Who knew Frank Hamilton? So far, no one had admitted to an acquaintance with the dead man.

He thought about Brookner's approach at the end of Edward Davenport's session. Gutsy, sure. But what had it accomplished? Why had the detective taken that approach? Jeff had told him he'd seen Hamilton arguing with a woman, not a man. Maybe he had uncovered something that he hadn't shared. Come to think of it, he hadn't shared anything. Maybe his former FBI status didn't mean a damn thing to Brookner.

He wondered if anyone had seen Frank Hamilton after he'd seen him last night at the edge of the Tea Garden. Of course, if he knew the answer to that . . . One thing he did know: The cops had a hell of a job ahead of them if they were going to question every woman who might have been wearing a little black dress. And a hat. Don't forget the hat.

The phone rang, jolting Jeff out of his thoughts.

"Found it," Blanche said by way of introduction.

"Where?"

"A place called the Murray Hotel."

Blanche gave him the number and made him promise to keep her posted.

"Will do." Jeff pressed the plunger, then punched in the number to the Murray. When the desk clerk answered, Jeff realized that he couldn't accomplish a damn thing over the phone. "Wrong number," he said, then hung up and located the place on his map.

Although the Murray Hotel was a large, clapboard structure on Main Street, he had trouble locating its entrance. The hotel's tiny porch abutted the sidewalk, and the people sitting there were close enough to touch. The only access to the porch was via a door behind the porch sitters. The hotel's entry was in an alcove next to that. He glanced at the faces to make sure Trudy wasn't on the porch, and then made his way to the hotel's front door.

At first glance, the inside of the hotel appeared to be a Victorian candy shop, with striped wallpaper, borders of roses, spandrels, and a large glass case that held several varieties of fudge. Had he known that, he could've saved a few stops and shopped here. Across from the fudge case was a carved oak staircase, its walls lined with antique photographs. Next to the stairs was a coffee bar with small tables and chairs. He walked past this, beyond the front desk, and down a corridor that led past the pay phones to the elevators.

Elevator. There was only one. He doubled back to the coffee bar.

Jeff figured the Murray's rooms would be less expensive than the Grand but, nonetheless, they were probably more than Trudy was used to spending. Of course, he had no idea how much money she had or if she had many financial responsibilities, but she looked like the poster girl for American Frugal and Trust.

He debated what approach to take. Too much time had passed since his years with the bureau. His investigative skills needed honing.

He ordered hazelnut coffee, grabbed an abandoned newspaper, and took up position at the back of the seating area. This way he could watch as guests came and went. He felt sure that everyone could see through the facade.

To his surprise, no one seemed to. Mackinac Island exuded security, and visitors there quickly became embraced within its guardian folds.

After a half hour, Trudy Blessing shuffled past him toward the elevator, juggling two grocery bags, a purse, and a half-eaten ice cream cone. She didn't look in his direction. If she had, she probably wouldn't have been able to identify him.

He felt guilty not offering to help. But, for the greater cause, he had to keep his low profile a little longer. When she disappeared into the elevator, he quickly climbed the stairs and watched for the lift to stop on the second floor. When it didn't, he hustled up another flight. He caught a glimpse of Trudy's yellow print skirt and a brown sandal as she turned right at the end of a long, narrow hallway.

He went after her. The walls were painted a dusty pink, and several Victorian photographs in period frames hung along the walls. At the end of the corridor, he stopped. Carefully, he peered around the corner. The walls in that wing were painted blue. At least the colors seemed like Trudy colors. She was fumbling with her key at a room directly across from a tall, old mirror.

When she stepped inside, he hurried to the door. Jeff knocked, heard a slight gasp from the other side. Skittish.

"Yes?" Her voice was trembling.

"Miss, I'm afraid something fell from one of your bags." He rustled his map, adding to the deceit.

"Oh, no. Just a moment, please."

He'd been right. Someone like Trudy would easily accept the implication that she'd dropped something.

She opened the door. When she saw Jeff, her breath caught and she tried to slam the door.

He pushed past her.

"Trudy, you're too trusting. Be thankful it's only me."

The girl fidgeted. "Mr. Talbot, how did you find me?"

"Never mind that for now. What in the hell are you doing here?"

"I don't have to answer that." Her lips tightened, as if to show that she'd zipped them. After a moment, she sat in an arm-chair and took a tiny birdcage from the small table beside her. As she studied it, her facade drooped. "I'm sorry if I sound disrespectful, but —"

"Don't apologize." He sat on the bed and looked around the room. It was small, only a fraction of the size of his suite, but it was done up with a rich Victorian theme in ivory and pink. The furniture was reproduction but still striking with its dark cherry finish. The only antiques were two more miniature birdcages. He picked them up. Trudy started to rise, then stayed put.

"Are these yours?" Jeff admired the crafts-manship in the tiny pieces.

"Yes. Seems silly, doesn't it? A grown woman traveling with birdcages. I don't even own a bird."

"I don't think it's silly at all. Lots of people travel with comfort items. Do you collect miniatures?"

"I collect birdcages in all sizes. The little ones are easy to bring along."

"What got you started collecting bird-cages?"

"I —" She stopped herself. "Are we through here, Mr. Talbot?"

"You took me by surprise, Trudy. You're the last person I expected to see here." Well, not the *last* person. That slot went to Sheila, hands down.

Trudy didn't respond.

Jeff went to the window and opened the blinds. "This is a great view. Have you looked out here?" Directly in front of him was the harbor, dotted with sailboats. Below, he could see the street scene. Delivery wagons hauled freight from the docks, people walked or rode bikes or just stood there watching the boats.

She stood and joined him. "It is nice, isn't it?"

"Are you here alone?"

A flash of panic showed in her eyes, then dissipated. He wasn't sure whether it meant she was hiding someone or if an admission of traveling alone would leave her vulnerable. "Trudy, you can trust me. If you don't believe that, then call Blanche. Now, tell me what's going on."

"There's only one toothbrush in the bathroom, Mr. Talbot," she said defensively. "Go check if you like."

Jeff didn't move.

"Really," she added, "I just needed some days off. When I overheard you talking about this place yesterday, I decided to be spontaneous, do something out of character. I work terribly hard for Mrs. Appleby, and I've never done very much for myself."

"You'll get no argument from me on that one. But why didn't you tell Blanche where you were going?"

"I suppose I didn't see any reason to."

"I know you rarely take vacations, but when you do, you always leave her a number, just in case there's a problem at the shop." He sat back down on the bed. "It's strange that you didn't this time."

"I — I guess I just didn't think of it. Besides, I wasn't sure where I'd be staying."

Jeff reached into three of the vest's pockets before he found his pad and pen. He jotted something, then tore the sheet out and handed it to her. "I'm staying at the Grand. But you probably already know that. Here's the number. Call me if you need anything, okay?"

"Yes, Mr. Talbot, I will."

Jeff placed the birdcages back on the table. "You know, Trudy, I'm surprised you aren't taking part in the Antiques Festival at the Grand."

"Like I said, this was a last-minute trip."

Jeff figured he'd pushed as far as he could. He said good-bye and stepped out the door. He was sure Trudy Blessing was up to something, but there was nothing more he could do right now to find out what.

He made his way around the boardwalk and back up toward his hotel, thinking about Trudy's explanations. He tried turning them different ways but couldn't come up with anything.

A siren blared, and he caught a glimpse of an ambulance as it shot up the street a couple of blocks over. Panic quickly gripped him, then reason told him to calm down. There were thousands of people on the island, what with the tourist trade out in full force today. It could mean nothing more than someone falling from his bike and fracturing an arm.

Slowly he climbed the hill that led up to the hotel. Lack of sleep from the night before was catching up to him. Maybe he could take a nap before afternoon tea.

He heard his name and looked up. Coming down the hill toward him was Lily Chastain, relying heavily on her cane as she leaned backward, counterbalancing herself so as not to topple headfirst down the steep hill.

"Jeffrey, how nice to see you."

"Mrs. Chastain." He nodded, tried to smile.

"It's Lily, remember?" She studied him. "What's wrong, dear?"

She pitched slightly. Jeff reached out and steadied her, then kept his palm cupped around her elbow for support. "My apologies, Lily. It's been a rather bizarre day."

"Yes, it has. Did you hear the dreadful news? Someone was found floating in Esther Williams's swimming pool."

Jeff smiled. He supposed anyone who'd actually been around when *This Time for Keeps* was filmed in 1947 would always look at the pool as belonging to the Olympic star and actress. "Actually, Lily, it was in the Tea Garden fountain."

"The *fountain?*" she said doubtfully. "Well, they do say a body can drown in an inch of water." She shook her head, then continued. "I would think, though, that a body would have to be trying awfully hard, wouldn't you?"

He nodded his agreement. "Unless, of course, the body had help."

Her eyes grew wide. "You don't really think . . . ?" she started. "This is Mackinac Island, for heaven's sake. There's no crime here. Now, take New Orleans — that's where I'm from, you see — now, New Orleans, it has its crime. The girls — Ruth Ann and Asia — and I check on each other every day of the world. Can you imagine a body not being found in that heat and humidity? Why —"

"Lily," Jeff interrupted. He hated to seem rude, but she'd spewed out all the sentences without so much as a breath in between. "Where *are* the girls?" He immediately felt strange for trying to get away with Lily's use of *girls*.

"They're both napping. I'm used to gardening at home. I like the great outdoors. The room seemed stuffy, so I thought I'd go for a little walk."

"I think I'll go back to the hotel and try

for one of those naps."

"The hotel? Oh, dear." She touched his arm. "I should have mentioned it when I first saw you. There's been another accident."

"Accident? What happened?"

"I'm not really sure. There were so many people crowding around, you know."

"I think I'll go check it out." Jeff told Lily to be careful maneuvering the hill, then excused himself and trotted to the crest of the hill. Flickering lights from an ambulance interrupted the scenery like a wild heartbeat in an unconscious soul.

Jeff was winded by the time he reached the Parlor.

Detective Brookner was standing at the elevator. He turned, saw Jeff, and slapped an arm up to keep the door from closing. "Talbot, come on."

Jeff stepped inside. "What's going on?"

Brookner punched a button, and the doors slid shut. "You tell me. That fella who was teaching the seminar this morning? Davenport? He just hung himself off the balcony of his room."

Chapter Seventeen

As Jeff walked down the third-floor corridor with Brookner, he saw paramedics wheel a gurney out of a room at the west end. Lieutenant Mel Littlefield stood outside the door, waiting. When the paramedics were clear, she slapped yellow police tape across the entry, then ducked underneath it and went inside.

Jeff wondered how the hotel's owners would react to the tape slashed across the room's entrance. It looked like a scar, one that put him in mind of something from his distant past.

He'd been making cold calls, stopping at farmhouses and in small-town neighborhoods to see if anyone might have "junk" he wanted to get rid of, when in an attic he'd come across a blanket chest. It had been made in America in the early 1800s and still wore its original black pigment with a Dutch folk art design in muted yellows and reds. Frantically, yet carefully, he had begun clearing the items stacked on its top.

His heart sank when he found the gash (it was too deep to be called a scratch). He ran his fingers along the raw yellow flesh of the

156

pine that had so recently been exposed. To find the disfigurement cut him to the quick. He searched for the culprit, for that item which had been so carelessly raked across the surface, but he couldn't find it. He questioned the owner, but the guy just kept asking what the big deal was. It drove Jeff's investigative instincts nuts, as if a criminal were lurking somewhere.

He'd purchased the wounded piece for ten bucks and had taken it home and daubed the cut with linseed oil. Since then, he'd been offered five figures for it — without the gash it would've easily brought six — but he could never bring himself to part with it. It was his personal reminder that every piece of American history has a soul.

That, he decided, was how the owners would feel about the yellow scar.

Jeff wasn't the only one who looked at antique furniture as human, and with good reason. Consider, for instance, a handcrafted Queen Anne secretary. Its shell is called a carcass. Its legs have knees, shins, feet. It has curves, movement, flow. As the cabinetmaker shaped it, it took on some of the man's spirit, his personality. It was no wonder, then, that the trade had a phrase that referred to those well-known or much-desired pieces floating around the antique world.

It was called "keeping track of the bodies."

Keeping track of human bodies was becoming a challenge at the Grand. Body number one wasn't cold yet, and now number two was being wheeled past Jeff and Brookner. Jeff recognized the two paramedics as those from the fountain that morning. They slowed, but Brookner showed no sign of stopping, so they resumed their pace.

Brookner ducked under the tape. Jeff followed.

Littlefield closed the door and stood guard. Jeff held back, took in the scene. The room was decorated in a tropical theme with splashes of orange, yellow, red, and green. That made it easy to pick out the forensics team.

Two Caucasian males in their midthirties and wearing gray suits were at the desk, leafing through stacks of papers, folders, books, even the telephone directory. A woman in a white lab coat over gray slacks and sweater was having a quiet conversation on a cell phone while a bald man in white lab coat and gray trousers wore surgical gloves as he dusted the room's phone for prints. As the man concentrated, his forehead split into five straight lines that put Jeff in mind of a musical staff.

The woman cursed, then punched a button and dropped the cell phone — it was no bigger than a powder compact — into a pocket on her coat. Jeff guessed her to be about thirty. Her brown hair was wound in a tight bun secured at the nape of her neck with two red pencils. A third pencil was parked over her right ear, and she grabbed it and began jotting notes on a clipboard.

One of the suits muttered something to the other, who in turn barked, "Then look again, damn it," and the first one shrugged and started another trek through the stacks.

Brookner checked his watch, then said to the woman, "Don't give up, Nic. You've got twenty long minutes till kickoff."

"Go square to hell, Brookner." She turned then, as if to check whether he'd vanished in a poof of purgatory-bound smoke, before continuing the conversation. The look changed to contempt when she saw Jeff. "This isn't a sideshow, mister."

She shot a look at Mel that said the lieutenant should do her job better, but before Mel could defend herself, Brookner said, "Stop sweet-talkin' the FBI, Nic. They don't take to it."

"Since when do we need FBI for suicide?"

"We don't. But this one's been kind of handy. Jeff Talbot, Nicole Whitney."

"The only way he'll be handy is if he's got a suicide note on him."

"I hadn't planned on needing one, Miss Whitney."

"That's reassuring, Mr. Talbot. I wonder if our Mr. Davenport planned his suicide. If he did, he sure as hell didn't let us know why."

"No note, huh?" Brookner said.

"Nope. If there were, do you think I'd still be here?"

"Point taken." Brookner gave the room the once-over. "What have you found?"

"The only thing worth mentioning is this." She produced a Ziploc bag. In it was a prescription bottle full of pink pills.

"Davenport took one of those at dinner last night," Jeff said. "With champagne."

"Not smart," said Whitney. "This is Tegretol. Among other things, it's used for treating bipolar disorder."

"Manic depression?" Brookner examined the full bottle. "Wonder why he didn't use these to check out with?"

Whitney grunted. "And deny me the pleasure of his swollen tongue and soiled suit?"

Brookner grinned. "I'm going downstairs where I can inhale some nicotine. For some reason, I always need a smoke after I talk to you."

The ME smiled for the first time. "I'll take that as a compliment, Detective."

The interrogation room looked pretty much the same as it had earlier, only there were a lot more folders on the desk.

Brookner motioned Jeff to a chair, then lowered himself into the one behind the desk with a heaviness that said he'd had to plant his butt there one too many times. He lit a cigarette and sucked in his fix. "Talbot." The word escaped with the smoke. "What did the FBI teach you about situations like this?"

"Like what? Murder? Suicide? They said to avoid them."

"Smart-ass." He sighed wearily. "You know, Talbot, your mug is showing up in a little too many scenarios connected to this case. I think you'd better start cooperating."

"My apologies, Detective. Murder's not a federal crime, unless it's the president, vice-president, or a member of Congress, so my training is different from yours. I have been giving this case a lot of thought, though. We're not going to get very far until we come up with some connections."

"We, huh?"

Jeff grinned. "Old habit, I guess. If it's okay with you I'd like to check with one of my old FBI buddies, see if I can turn up any common bonds."

"You do that. As long as you understand that I'm first on your snitch list. Understood?"

Jeff nodded. "Hasn't questioning the guests turned up anything?"

"Not so far. Pieces here and there, but none of them fit together. Not yet, anyway."

"What about Hamilton's room? Anything there?"

"The usual stuff: shaving kit, some old suitcases, couple books."

"Mind if I take a look? Sometimes people in my line of work find ingenious ways of hiding things."

Brookner pondered this offer. At length, he shrugged. "Oh, what the hell. I got no problem with it, so long as you don't go telling any cops that I'm cooperating with the FBI." A crystal ashtray had been placed on the desk since Jeff's last time to the room. Brookner balanced his cigarette on it, then located a manila envelope with Hamilton written across it in red block letters and fished out a key. He tossed it to Jeff.

Mel Littlefield walked in without knocking. Apparently they'd dispensed with formalities in the interest of time. "Detective, Callie here says she saw our necktie expert talking with Hamilton last night."

Brookner slapped the top of the desk and said, "Now we're getting somewhere."

Jeff stood and offered his chair to the woman. She waved him off.

She was black, large boned and stocky, and had that same ageless quality Jeff had observed earlier in Lieutenant Littlefield. He wondered whether it was the dark-skinned heritage or the extra weight that gave this ageless illusion. Caucasian women cooked their skin for the dark effect, which only negated their attempts at youth by adding wrinkles. But too much money had been spent in the war against fat for women to change their minds at this late date.

Jeff made a mental note to invest in America's diet industry.

Callie's crisp housekeeping uniform was a gray dress with a starched white collar and matching cuffs. A white apron and well-cushioned white shoes completed the outfit. Jeff wondered whether the maids dressed in neutral tones in order to pick one another out from their bright surroundings.

Brookner pulled a pen from his pocket. "Tell me what you saw."

"Yes, sir. It was around eight o'clock in the evening." It was obvious that English was her second language. She took great care with pronunciation and spent a little more time on the *N*s, creating the illusion of liquid flowing. "I was providing turn-down service on the third floor. Most folks are downstairs to dinner during that time, so we knock a couple of times, then let ourselves in, turn down the bedding, and put chocolates on the pillows."

"Chocolates."

"Yes, sir." She reached in her apron's pocket and brought out a miniature square envelope with a moon and stars and the Grand Hotel nestled in a bed of clouds. Scripted alongside was the greeting, "Sweet Dreams." It was just like the one Jeff had found on his pillow last night. "Want one?" She passed them out to all of us. "They's not bad," she added, her proper English slipping slightly.

Brookner studied the little packet.

"Eight?" Jeff looked at Brookner. "That's about the time Davenport was called away from dinner."

Brookner's brows raised accusingly.

"Let me explain. I'd been invited to dinner by Ben and Jennifer Hurst. They mentioned that they were dining with a friend. I decided it beat eating alone." He thought about adding that it hadn't, but the jury was still out. "Anyway, around eight, a hotel messenger approached the table and handed Davenport a note. He was upset after he read it, said something about a glitch with the auction plans. He left in a big hurry."

Brookner turned to Littlefield. "Get the Hursts in here."

Littlefield started toward the door.

"And see if somebody can track down the messenger who delivered that note to Davenport last night."

"Can I go, too?" Callie asked anxiously. Littlefield waited while the maid continued. "Belinda's so upset that she can't work, and I've got to cover her."

"Upset?" Brookner said. "Why?"

"She's the one who found that man with a belt around his neck."

"Littlefield —"

"Got it, boss. I'll bring her, too."

After Jeff was dismissed, he fought the urge to go to Hamilton's room and went instead to his own.

He needed to put his FBI source and long-time fishing buddy, Gordon Easthope, to work on some background checks. Jeff was a master of the contingency plan and always traveled with contact information on a variety of sources, from FBI to antiques experts to an encoded list on a subculture of people who had proven indispensable during his time with the bureau.

He looked up a number in his address book and picked up the phone. A sense of déjà vu came with it. When he'd worked as a desk jockey, he'd gotten so damned tired of having a phone screwed to his ear. He'd be glad when this death business was wrapped up so he could concentrate on finding antiques and on getting that cabaret set for Blanche. He punched numbers.

A deep bass identified itself as Easthope.

"Gordy? What are you doing answering your own phone? Did you sprout a heart and give Joan the day off?"

"Like hell. You didn't go *that* far east, Talbot. It's Saturday here, too."

"Saturday?" Jeff sighed wearily. "I guess you're right. Feels like I've been here for a hell of a lot longer than one day."

"Sounds like it, too. What did you do? Get

up early and pull in a few trout?"

"Haven't even had a chance."

"You're missing a bet. Michigan's a fishing paradise. What about the treasure hunting?"

"Getting interrupted by murder, mostly."

"Yeah? At an antique convention? What happened, did you kill some guy who outbid you, or did some female wallop the gal next to her so she could make off with the goods? That happens all the time at Macy's."

"I found the first body. Turns out it's another picker from Seattle."

"You know him?"

"You could say that. Matter of fact, I had a run-in with him a couple of days ago."

"Trying to clear your own name then."

"I guess you could say that." Jeff started jotting names on the yellow pad by the phone.

"Wait a minute. You said 'first body.' How many you got?"

"Two. Second one's suicide."

"Is it? Or does it just look that way?"

"Only thing missing is a note," Jeff said ironically.

"Uh-huh." Gordy's tone was heavy with skepticism. "Notes are iffy at best. People fake 'em or force a guy to sign some type-written piece of crap. What you need is motive, my friend, whether you're dealing with murder or suicide."

Although Gordy had been with the Bureau

for more than twenty years, he'd begun his career with the Dallas Police Department. Jeff's own deduction skills had been honed by Gordy, his mentor and long-time friend.

"Listen, Gordy. There's a George Lawrence creel here with your name on it if you'll run a few checks for me, see what the system spits out." Jeff was always on the lookout for fishing memorabilia — decoys, lures, creels, anything fishy — to add to Gordy's collection.

"You're kidding." The muffled screech of Gordy's ancient but broken-in desk chair came over the line. Jeff knew the man had jumped to his feet. "Tooled leather?"

"You know it."

"Brass plate, too?"

"Yep."

"I've been looking for that one since Papa fished Walloon Lake." When Gordy said "Papa," he was referring to his favorite fisherman and author — in that order — Ernest Hemingway. He'd always claimed it was too endearing a term to be wasted on his own deadbeat dad.

When Gordy continued, his tone was more reserved. "Hell, you know that. You'll bring it to me anyway, just because you think you can rob an old man blind. Hang on." Jeff could hear paper rattling, then Gordy continued. "I'm in. Shoot."

Jeff rattled off the list he'd just written —

surprised, suddenly, that it was a list. When he was through, he said, "Leave a message if I'm not in the room. Brookner — that's the detective heading up the investigation — gave me a key to Hamilton's room. I'm headed there now to see if anything was overlooked."

"Key, huh?" Gordy grunted. "Yeah, it sounds like you're one of their prime suspects, all right."

"You always told me I have an honest face."

"Yeah, as long as you hold that outdated federal ID in front of it."

"What can I say? Most people think FBI stands for Fanatical But Innocent."

"They must." Gordy hung up.

Chapter Eighteen

Frank Hamilton's room was near the west end of the Parlor level. Jeff started down the corridor, noting a brass plate with a number that told him he had a walk ahead of him. As he strode down the corridor, he also noted that all the doors were alike: massive white slabs that looked more like entrances to columned mansions. These guarded rooms were as different from one another as a Regency sideboard was from a Shaker washstand. He hurried along, keeping an eye out for another yellow scar. There wasn't one, and he almost shot past the room. This surprised him, until he realized the police tape wouldn't be here. Hamilton was dead, but he hadn't been killed in his room.

The brass oval plate that hung beside the door and identified the room almost escaped Jeff's attention. It had been polished recently, and as he slid the key into the hole he angled himself in order to cut the glare and see what was engraved upon the disk. An elegant script read Napoleon Suite.

An instant of confusion, followed by a flash of envy. Was it possible? Had he missed the opportunity to stay in this suite because of Frank Hamilton, a guy who probably didn't give a damn about atmosphere?

Jeff opened the door and slipped inside. He flipped the light switch and stood there for several moments while the atmosphere permeated his senses.

Bonaparte would have complained. Not because of the decorating, which at first glance was true to the empire's clarets and golds and black lacquers. The emperor, in spite of his slight stature, would have groused for want of more floor space to spread his maps and get belly down among them like a child playing engineer with a toy train set.

Jeff walked around. It wasn't a suite in the true sense of the word, but it had obviously earned that status by way of sheer decadence. Rich claret paper covered the walls in a design that mimicked festooned silk. Above that, gilded molding framed the room. The bedding and draperies were in rich claret tones and heavy with gold satin passementerie, from the corded ropes to the yards and yards of bullion fringe. A massive oval mirror, antique and gilded and worth more than everything else in the room combined, dominated one wall.

The bed was made. Jeff wondered if housekeeping had been in. He remembered then that Hamilton had likely never slept in it. Even if the cops had checked under the layers of bedspread and sheets, someone had followed them and made it up again.

A French Empire commode, heavily gilded, stood between a pair of black lacquered Empire side chairs upholstered in claret damask and embroidered with the Emperor's trademark bees. The stark, linear Empire style was evident from top to bottom: Art, figurines, furniture, carpets, each and every detail had been painstakingly attended to.

Why would Frank Hamilton choose this suite?

As Jeff pondered this, a suspicion of the young picker's reason for being at the festival began to worm its way into his mind.

Frank Hamilton had come here to acquire the cabaret set.

Realizing this, Jeff knew it would lead, somehow, to the young man's killer. It might also lead to the reason behind the death of the auctioneer, a death that could as likely be murder as suicide.

All he had to do was prove it.

He got to work. The jewelry roll he'd brought along worked perfectly for storing his traveling tools. He pulled the grosgrain ties and unwrapped the padded fabric. From the stitched compartments, he chose a snake light and looped it around his neck so that his hands would be free while he searched. Next, he took out the telescoping mirror and put it in one of his pockets. It would be used to check under and behind furniture, and would prevent his having to move any heavy pieces.

He flipped the snake light's switch and started his search in the bathroom. The room seemed an afterthought, compared to the opulence of the suite. It was a modern bathroom with your basic white porcelain and tile. He checked between the folds of the towels and in the tank of the toilet. He checked under the countertop and behind the shower curtain. He unscrewed the shower head but only got a splash of water in his face for his trouble. On the marble countertop was a shaving kit, which appeared to be the only item that hadn't come with the room and proved nothing more than the fact that Hamilton brushed and flossed and shaved. He traveled with none of the contingency things Jeff always took along: aspirin, bandages, cold medicine, styptic pencil, burn cream.

Jeff moved back to the main area of the suite. A white terrycloth robe with the Grand Hotel's monogram of a Hackney-pulled carriage in green had been slung carelessly over a chaise longue upholstered in burgundy silk. Jeff snatched it up, knowing that, if it was wet, it would ruin the delicate fabric. When he checked, though, he found that both the chair and the robe were dry. Actually, he would have been surprised if Hamilton had been so careless. The young man had exhibited a respect for antiques when he'd stroked the pram in Jeff's car only two days before.

Jeff examined two books about antiques that were on one of the nightstands. The Bulfinch volume was one Jeff considered indispensable. The second, familiar to him as well, was about English and continental porcelain. He had to credit Hamilton with knowing his stuff; both volumes were highly regarded in the business.

Jeff was nothing if not thorough, and he was sure Brookner's crew was the same. Jeff went through the motions anyway, checking behind paintings, in potted plants, under lamps, *in* lamps, beneath tables. He was almost amazed to find that no gum was stuck under the tables. He wondered if the maids had to check regularly for such signs of disrespect to the fine antiques.

He checked for hollow legs and hollow bedposts. He pulled every drawer from every chest and table, looking for hidden packets that might be taped underneath. Using his mirror and light, he peered underneath and behind every stick of furniture in the room. He examined the backs of mirrors and paintings to see if they'd recently been removed. He scrutinized the drapery hems for threads that either didn't match or that were stitched differently from the original tailor's handiwork.

The "old suitcases," as Brookner had called them, were two vintage crocodile valises in pristine condition. Jeff began with the largest. Carefully, he removed jeans and T-shirts, checking their pockets for contents. He checked the case for a false bottom. There wasn't one.

He went through the same procedure with the smaller case. In this one were under-clothes, a pair of swim trunks, and a pair of the Adidas sandals that soccer players wear off the field. They looked strange housed in the vintage case in an antique-filled room, as if the footwear were in the wrong century, rather than the other way around. Jeff checked again for a false bottom. Nothing.

He walked to each tabletop, examining fig-ures, knickknacks, every trinket that adorned every surface. He expected a figure of a woman seated on a garden bench to open up and reveal an inkwell, but when it didn't, he only sighed and dropped into a chair beside the table on which it rested.

Against the wall at the back of the table was a fabulous Empire mantel clock in bronze. Lavishly ornamented, it resembled a shadowbox more than it did a clock. It was a miniature parlor, with a young maiden seated at a piano, her fingers positioned on the keys. Behind her were windows, elegantly draped and looking not unlike those in the suite. Golden griffins stood guard at the corners.

Three more griffins stood under the piano and served as legs, their wings supporting the weight of the instrument.

He'd seen a photo of the clock somewhere and believed the magnificent piece was the work of Raviro. On a whim, he reached out, hooked the tip of his index finger under the lip of the piano's diminutive lid, and lifted. It was hinged. He raised it. An accordioned slip of paper popped up like a jack-in-the-box.

Jeff adjusted the snake light, aiming its beam onto the paper. It was some sort of document — rather, a photocopy of a document because the seal was flat and gray. The original would have been a disk of gold or silver foil. Certificate, diploma, it was hard to tell. In German, he believed, but he couldn't be sure.

Something deep inside him said he should call Brookner. He didn't listen.

It didn't seem like much to go on, but he knew who might be able to help.

He started out the door, then paused and looked up at a painting on the wall. Napoleon looked back approvingly from his vantage point atop a majestic steed.

Jeff rushed to his room, his mind racing with plans and possibilities. He didn't know much about Internet investigation. While he was active with the Bureau, he'd relied on an assistant at headquarters to invest the necessary time needed to track things down via the world wide web. Jeff's take on the Internet was that it consumed an inordinate amount of time if one didn't keep it in check. Mostly, while he was home, he and Sheila spent much quality time together, visiting about their many interests, sharing the events of the day, watching movies or television, or just sitting in the library reading, secure in the knowledge that the other was in the same room enjoying the same pastime.

There were times, however, when his wife was on-line for hours, researching something of interest or participating in chats or keeping an eye on her bids at eBay. He didn't begrudge her these times, because it comprised the lion's share of her interaction with other people. But it was a part of technology he'd never had much use for.

He snatched the phone from its cradle and punched his home number.

"Is this the man who stood me up for breakfast?" Sheila asked. She loved caller ID and usually didn't waste time with preambles.

"Honey, I'm sorry about how things ended last night. But I'm not sorry for missing you."

"Fair enough. That doesn't change the fact that you were supposed to call this morning. I was beginning to think I'd been replaced by antiques."

"Not in a million years." Jeff told her

about the deaths of Frank Hamilton and Edward Davenport. He filled her in on the call to Gordy and concluded with the discovery of the document he now held in his hand.

"Jeff, do you think you're safe?"

"What? Oh, sure. Don't worry about me."

"I can't help it. Promise me you'll watch your back."

"Always. Anyway, hon, I've got Gordy running background checks on some of the people attending the festival, but I wonder if you'd be willing to help on something international." He barely got the request out before she said yes. He knew she'd love playing virtual detective. "I found a document of some sort. It's in German, I think — lots of umlauts and consonants crowded together like they've never met a vowel. I wonder what it's like to play *Wheel of Fortune* over there?"

"What?"

"Never mind. The name of the person who received the citation or diploma or whatever this is, is Eric Von Screibtisch. There's also a field that might be a company or an institution, or maybe his major or something — says 'Europaervolkswirtschaft'." He spelled the word.

Sheila repeated the spellings. "Are you sure there's nothing else on there I might need?"

"I don't speak German so, no, I'm not sure. Start with what I gave you, and we'll see if I need to translate the rest." He folded the paper and slid it into his pocket. "How are things there? Everything okay?"

"Sure. I found a salmon recipe in an old *Bon Appetit* that sounds fabulous, so I'm making that for dinner tonight. Greer went down to the fish market for fresh salmon."

"No cedar planks tonight?" Jeff asked. Much as Sheila loved to experiment with new recipes, she often used the time-honored Pacific Northwest tradition of grilling salmon on soaked cedar. Of course, that meant either Jeff or Greer had to do the outdoors cooking.

"No. The recipe I found has wild rice and dried cranberries. I hope you don't mind, but I'm using what Gordy had shipped to you from Cabela's last Christmas."

"That's fine. If it's a hit, will you make it for me when I get home?"

"If you'll catch the salmon."

"Sounds good. I'll be ready for a nice, relaxing fishing trip after this." Jeff stretched out on the bed. "Did you persuade Greer to join you for dinner?"

Sheila laughed. "Finally. It wasn't easy, though. I threatened to dine on peanut butter sandwiches if he left me to eat alone."

"Good girl. Granted, the food here is first class, but I'm missing your special touch."

"Are you still talking about my cooking?"

"Not now, I'm not." He sighed. "I miss you."

"Two-way street, Talbot."

It used to bother him when she put an edge back on things. He'd thought it cold and uncaring. But she had explained that it was the only way she could deal with the loneliness — by not wallowing in it. He suspected she'd offered that explanation in order to protect his feelings. He'd always been the romantic of the pair.

"Call me when you've got a German lesson for me."

"I will. Jeff?"

"Yeah?"

"Be careful, okay?"

"I knew you cared."

The red message light on the phone winked invitingly at him as soon as Jeff cradled the receiver. He accessed voice mail, then sat up and grabbed a pen when he heard Gordon Easthope's voice. Thankfully, he hadn't forgotten his own special form of shorthand. After years of working with Gordy, Jeff knew the man rattled off stats like he was announcing a Mariners game.

"Jeff, grab your Big Chief tablet. Here we go."

Jeff heard a shuffling of papers, then Gordy said, "Frank Hamilton, Seattle resident, six years, moved from Indy where he worked as a picker, never married.

"Edward Davenport, arrived in the US of

A from England eighteen years ago, has lived in the Big Apple ever since, foremost authority on English history — you probably know that already — no other information.

"Your Three Musketeers, namely Lily Chastain, Ruth Ann Longan, Asia Graham, all for one and one for all, and they've been that way since George Burns was smoking bubblegum see-gars, have resided in New Orleans over fifty years, all widowed, active in community service: hospital, theater, delivering Meals on Wheels. Considering their ages, shouldn't that be the other way around? Anyway, that's it on them.

"Benjamin Hurst, army brat, hopped all over the map till he enrolled at Ohio State University, employed by Grant Industries after graduation, married Jennifer Grant — the boss's daughter, looks like — about six years ago.

"Jennifer Hurst, yadda yadda University, ditto, Grant Industries. Right after they married, she and Hurst moved to Saint Paul from — wait, this is interesting . . ."

Jeff waited, heard more shuffling of papers, then Gordy's voice continued. "From Indianapolis. That was about six years ago."

"So?" Jeff said to the recorded message as he jotted "IND 6YR" next to "JH/GRANT."

"So," Gordy said as if answering him, "that means your Hursts and Body Number One — Hamilton — were in Indy at the same time. Long shot, but I'd better keep checking. I'll call you back."

Jeff punched Seven to erase the message and hung up. He looked over his notes. It could be nothing more than a coincidence. Hell, Indy's huge. But Gordy was right; they would need to learn whether there were any connections. Any connections at all.

Chapter Nineteen

The Parlor was crowded by the time Jeff arrived for afternoon tea. He worked his way through the knots of chattering people, picking up stray words as he went along that told him the deaths were the main topic of conversation.

He had changed into olive slacks and shirt, a sport coat in linen, and a vintage silk tie in muted shades of olive, ivory, black, and wine in a pattern that put one in mind of Havana palms and Panama hats. The cuff links, gold cigars with enameled bands, were from the forties.

He decided to find Brookner before Brookner found him. That way he could unload all the information he'd come up with and, he hoped, unload his mind a little so he could enjoy the festival for a few hours.

He checked the interrogation room, but the door was closed. There was a window looking out onto the hallway from the small office. The vertical blinds weren't completely closed, and Jeff could see the female cop, Mel Littlefield, talking to a staff member. He'd heard political correctness was seeping into some departments and that the term *interview room* was now being used. When he observed the stocky Indian woman in action, however, he decided interrogation wasn't an endangered species in this neck of the woods.

She saw him then and came out the door. "Don't you look *sharp*." She eyed him up and down. "Just like the new Kevin Spacey."

"New?"

"Yep. He musta got himself one of those Hollywood stylists. Dresses really snazzy now."

"Well, thanks. I think. He looks to me like a middle-aged guy with a receding hairline and jowls like a Basset hound."

"Not with those sexy eyes and new duds, he don't. You make me want to go home and watch *L.A. Confidential* or something."

He started to ask what the 'or something' might be, but he let it pass. Sometimes he missed the playful office banter that those in law enforcement relied upon. It was a vital way of maintaining sanity against the daily doses of stress and death.

She sighed. "Won't be watching movies tonight, though. This case is moving along just like the traffic around here: mighty slow, with a lot of stops for horseshit."

Jeff laughed. "Don't let me slow you down, then. I'm looking for Brookner. He around?"

"Should be back soon. Tell me where you'll be, and I'll have him look you up."

"The Parlor, miss, for afternoon tea." He pantomimed drinking with his pinkie extended.

"You're makin' me hungry for scones, Mr. Talbot." She curtsied and headed back into the interrogation room.

Long stretches of tables were placed end to end in the Parlor and dressed in crisp white linen. Pedestaled crystal cake stands and silver trays and compotes held a feast of delicacies: pastries, sandwiches, fruits. He thought of Sheila and how much she would appreciate the artistry. Suddenly, he realized that every time he saw a particularly stylized presentation of food, he thought of Sheila. *What was I like before her?*

He tried to remember. After a moment, he realized that no answer came to him. He simply couldn't recall life before Sheila. His adult life, anyway. His emotional life. His life as a man.

Easily enough, he remembered growing up with Auntie Pim and Grandfather after his parents were killed. The older Talbots had taught him about high tea and etiquette and proper dress for a gentleman. That was how antiques had first gotten into his blood. The house was full of them, things that were passed down from one generation to the next. And each generation had been taught to respect those heirlooms, to appreciate the history behind them, to keep them in the family. Early on, Jeff had begun adding to those collections and acquiring the accoutrements needed to carry out those rituals.

He'd started with grooming brushes, handsome sets that included brushes for hair, clothing, hats, boots. He had complete sets in every material imaginable: ebony, a wood with such heft it would sink in water; tortoise, so alive with character that he believed if he gripped it just so he could feel the pulse of the body behind the shell; carved horn and ivory; monogrammed sterling.

Silver clinked, snapping Jeff back to reality.

The general mood of this afternoon's tea crowd was subdued, compared to the gaiety of the previous night's cocktail party. The deaths had obviously had their effect on everyone.

When a server offered him a cup of tea, he asked instead for coffee. The server's brows raised ever so slightly, but he moved a gloved hand to another pot and poured. Jeff glared at the man, debating whether to ask why he had coffee if he was going to judge those drinking it. In the end, however, he decided not to waste his energy. He took two hefty drinks, prompted the waiter to refill the cup, and made his way across the room.

Ben and Jennifer Hurst were standing near the main entrance, looking as if they had just stepped out of *The Great Gatsby*. Jeff started to approach them, then held back. The two were lost in conversation, obviously in love, oblivious to the room full of people. They stood so physically close that each might have drunk from the other's cup as easily and deftly as his or her own. They fit like custom-made kid leather gloves, conforming to the unique shape of the hands for which they were crafted, gripping the thin, delicate web of skin between the fingers.

Ben's heather gray vintage trousers and buttoned vest put Jeff in mind of a young Robert Redford. A glittering gold watch chain hammocked loosely across his flat stomach. An ivory shirt, gold cuff links, and saddle oxfords in tan and brown finished the 1930s effect.

Jennifer wore a flowing dress in black printed with tiny pink tea roses. Its flared hem fluttered about her shapely calves in the breeze slipstreaming through the open doors. Her shoes were of black brocade with those chunky little hourglass heels. A tiny bag, beaded with jets, hung on her arm, and a vintage black cloche hid her eyes in profile.

Jeff reddened, feeling suddenly voyeuristic and very alone. He turned to leave.

As if she sensed him, Jennifer pivoted and called his name.

He turned back.

She smiled and motioned him over. "Where have you been hiding yourself?"

Jennifer slipped her arm through his, and

he was surprised at how comfortable he felt with the simple gesture that meant he was being included.

Ben gave Jeff's arm a slap. "We were afraid the local yokels had detained you."

"You may be closer to the truth than you realize." Jeff wondered then if the couple tended to be alone most of the time because people viewed them as unapproachable. They were the kind many judged upon first meeting as snobbish, pretentious, spoiled. Jeff was ashamed to admit that he'd leaned that way, too, in the beginning, even though he was totally comfortable with himself in social situations. Now, he almost felt sorry for the couple who came off as aloof merely because of their outer beauty. The Hursts were simply the sort of people who were comfortable with themselves. They seized life, making the best of all it had to offer. Others blamed people like Ben and Jennifer for their own failure at being able to adopt that positive attitude toward living. Filled with animosity, they either reacted with a snobbishness all their own or secretly envied them, proclaiming that they, too, would be like the Hursts once they moved up the corporate ladder or lost weight or married into money so as to afford the nip-and-tuck-and-sculpt-and-tan approach to popularity. Jeff believed the Hursts' appearances were simply the blessing of good genes.

Jennifer looked from Jeff to her husband,

then back. "We were just reveling in the good fortune that we're alive and have each other. You've no doubt heard about Edward." Her tone indicated genuine sorrow.

"Yes. Hard to believe."

"Impossible to believe is more like it," Ben said. "We don't buy into this suicide story. And no note? Come on."

"Did you attend his seminar this morning?" Jennifer asked. "Edward was his usual, charismatic self. It's beyond my comprehension to think he would suddenly take his own life after that."

"It was a powerful session," Jeff agreed, not wanting to share his feelings that it, like Davenport's dinner performance the evening before, seemed a little over the top. "I suppose anything's possible, but you're right about the note. It's never easy to buy into suicide if there's no indication as to why. I'm sure the police are checking on his family situation."

"There's not one, that we know of. Edward's always been a loner." Ben paused. "But let's face it. The police said that that Hamilton guy was killed. What if someone killed Edward, too?"

"It's something to consider. I'm sure the police haven't ruled it out."

"I would hope they haven't," Jennifer said. "Especially without a suicide note. Don't you think there would've been something to indicate why he did it? *If* he did it?"

Jeff finished his coffee. "You never know about some people. That's the only certainty when dealing with something like this. But to answer your question, yes. There's usually a clue as to why someone ends it like that."

"It's beginning to get scary." Jennifer moved closer to Ben. "Do you think we're safe staying here?"

Ben embraced her. "Sweetheart, if I thought we were in any danger, we'd leave right now. But I really think this is just some bizarre coincidence. Besides, the hotel has added extra security — something they didn't even have to do, what with all the cops around. We'll just stick together like we'd planned, okay?"

Jeff started to say something but paused when he saw Trudy Blessing weaving her way around small groups of people on the porch.

Crouched as she was, with her arms up and shoulders hunched, she looked as if she were sneaking through enemy lines. She maneuvered the last group and started through the doorway, then stopped abruptly. A look of fear clouded her face behind the large glasses, as if she'd just stumbled upon the battlefield itself.

"Trudy?" Jeff called.

She jumped, looked at him, then started to turn, but not before Ben and Jennifer turned toward her.

Trudy gasped, then went pale. She mur-

mured something — Jeff thought it was his name — but the look on her face and the sound of her voice both indicated confusion. She staggered, then turned and bolted.

"Trudy!" Jeff ran after her.

She moved faster than he expected. When he finally caught up to her, she was halfway down the hill that led away from the hotel. "Trudy, what the hell was that all about? You start to say my name, then you just run away? What's wrong?"

Trudy stopped, turned to face him. "No, Mr. Talbot."

As many times as he had asked her to call him Jeff, she'd always addressed him as Mr. Talbot. It didn't add up.

"Not *your* name." Trudy looked past him. "Hers."

Jeff spun around. He found himself face to face with Jennifer Hurst.

Chapter Twenty

Jeff felt as confused as Trudy looked. "You two know each other?"

Jennifer glanced at him briefly but didn't answer. She stepped around him and spoke to the young woman. "Trudy, I'm so sorry to be seeing you under these circumstances."

"What? What circumstances?"

Taking hold of one of Trudy's arms, Jennifer turned to Jeff. "She's in a state of shock. Help me get her inside."

Jeff gently took Trudy's other arm, although he had no idea why. "Shock from what?"

Trudy broke free of them both and set her feet. "I'm not a child, and I would appreciate it if you'd both stop treating me like one. What on earth is going on?"

"If you don't know what's —" Jennifer stopped. "Why are you here, Trudy?"

"I was supposed to meet Frank, but he never showed up. Which, as you well know, is typical of him. Why do I keep letting myself get roped into his schemes? Well, whether anyone believes it or not, I came here to tell him to forget it. I came here to tell him that

I wasn't going to help him anymore. But the phones have been busy here all afternoon — you'd think they would add more lines if they have that many calls —"

"Frank? Frank who? Hamilton?" Jeff's mind was reeling. He wanted to catch up to speed, but he wasn't sure which lane to follow.

Trudy stared at him, wide-eyed behind the saucer-like glasses.

"Wait a minute," Jeff said. "You know Frank Hamilton?"

No one spoke.

He nodded then. "I guess that's not as crazy as it sounds. I mean, you're both in the antique business, you both live, or —"

Lived, he started to correct himself. Then it dawned on him.

Jennifer gasped. "Oh, no. Trudy, you don't know, do you? Sweetie, Frank was killed this morning."

"What?" Trudy fell backward, as if the wind had been knocked out of her. Jeff grabbed for her as she slumped to the ground. He barely managed to break her fall.

Jennifer was instantly beside the girl, speaking softly and stroking her hair. She turned to Jeff. "Help me get her to my room."

They entered the east end of the hotel, choosing a path that would help them avoid the crowded Parlor. The trio — tiny, frail Trudy, flanked by Jeff and Jennifer — ascended the flight of stairs beside the information desk, then took the elevator to the fourth floor.

Once inside her room, Jennifer tossed key, purse, and hat onto a table and focused completely on Trudy. As she settled the girl into bed, Jeff got a glass of water and a washcloth and brought them to Jennifer.

She held the glass for Trudy, then gently bathed the girl's face with the cool, wet cloth.

Jeff lowered himself onto a tufted satin love seat and waited.

The brass plate Jeff had seen outside the door identified this as the Rosalyn Carter Suite. The walls were of peach satin, an obvious nod to the former First Lady's beloved Georgia. The carpet was a deep, rich blue and woven with creamy white stars in a circular pattern representing the presidential seal.

The bed, the armoire, the dressing table with its white marble top were a set fashioned from rosewood and ornately carved in the rococo revival style. It was just like the set used by his Auntie Pim, which still occupied her old bedroom in the house where he now lived. It was authentic Prudent Mallard.

"Trudy is Frank's sister," Jennifer began. "We all lived in Indianapolis until six or seven years ago." She stopped, gave Trudy another drink. "Seems much longer ago than that."

Jeff stared, unbelieving. Had he not been sitting when this news was delivered, he probably would have fallen down. Trudy and Frank *siblings?* They'd done a hell of a job keeping it a secret. He thought about Blanche then. Did she know? If so, wouldn't she have told him? Especially in light of his call to her earlier? It had been only a few hours ago that he'd phoned Blanche, told her about Hamilton's murder and Trudy's presence on the island. Brother and sister. Was that something Trudy would have — *could have* — kept from Blanche?

"Jeff?" Jennifer's voice was sharp. "Did you hear me? I said, I think she's in shock."

She's not the only one. "I'll call a doctor."

"No. No doctor." Trudy was shivering. "I'll be fine."

Jeff retrieved a woven throw from the couch and layered it onto the comforter Jennifer had already pulled over the girl. He snugged it up under her chin, then sat on the edge of the bed. "How about something a little stronger to drink?"

"No, I really shouldn't."

"He's right, Trudy." Jennifer opened the wet bar, retrieved a miniature bottle of cognac, and twisted the cap off with a snap. She poured its contents into a glass and held it to the girl's lips.

Trudy took a sip. She wheezed and coughed when the fumes hit, shaking her head and pushing the glass away.

"More, Trudy," Jennifer said firmly. Trudy drank without further prompting.

Jeff studied Jennifer. This was a much different side of her. Of course, this was a very different situation. But you never knew with people like Jennifer — what little he knew of her, anyway — how they would respond during a crisis. He was impressed to see that she'd put aside the bubbly celebrity act. He thought about how she hadn't denied knowing Trudy, hadn't tried to cover up with defensive excuses. It said a great deal about her character.

Jennifer turned to Jeff. "How is it you two know each other?"

Jeff told her about Blanche and All Things Old. "Trudy will deny it, but she's Blanche's right arm at the shop."

"Trudy, I had no idea you were living in Seattle."

"That's where Frank lived, too," Jeff added.

Jennifer looked up at him for a moment, then back at Trudy. At length, she continued her story. "I'd just graduated from Ohio State and moved back to Indianapolis. I went to work for my father's company and got a loft apartment in this fabulously renovated old building. Trudy lived there, too. She was one of the first people I met.

"She introduced me to Frank. She didn't want to, but I pushed her until she did." She looked at Trudy. "Turns out I should've listened to you, right, sweetie?"

Trudy smiled slightly. Her eyes were already going glassy.

Jennifer removed Trudy's glasses and told her to get some rest. She stood, looked down at Jeff. "I could use one of those drinks myself. Would you like one?"

"Sounds good." Jeff patted Trudy's arm, then moved back to the love seat. "How close can you come to a bona fide martini?"

"Makeshift. No olives. No shaker. Can you handle it, Bond?"

"As long as it's gin, not vodka."

"That I can manage."

Jennifer stooped at the small refrigerator, juggled tiny bottles, then surfaced and began mixing. "Frank charmed me to the core. I felt pampered, protected, desired. He completely swept me off my feet. I must've been going through a James Dean phase or something. You know, drawn to that rebel attitude, that raw sexiness." She handed Jeff a glass with clear liquid, then joined him on the couch and took a drink of what he figured was a screwdriver. A mimosa, however, would have been more in keeping with her high tea outfit.

"One day," she went on, "I suddenly, frighteningly, realized I had given up my *self*:

my opinions, my freedom, my identity. To this day, I don't know how he got his hooks into me. What's worse is that I don't know why I allowed it.

"I'd seen how he was with Trudy — bossy, controlling, manipulative — and I had even tried to talk to her about it. But he was her big brother, and she didn't have any other family to speak of. She made excuses for him, said it was because he cared for her so much. The same excuses I'd been using."

Jeff thought about Trudy's birdcage collection and how appropriate it was that she should choose an item so symbolic of incarceration.

Jennifer took a drink. "Best thing I ever did was get away from him. It took me a while to get over him and what he did to me. I had nightmares and paranoia, then moved on to a sort of denial — a separation of that person from the one I was trying to become.

"When I first met Ben, I didn't want to trust anyone. He certainly had his work cut out for him. Eventually, though, I discovered how different the two were and . . ." She shrugged.

"This morning, when I heard Frank was dead, all those emotions flashed through me, through my senses. Then an enormous relief washed over me. Not that he was dead — he wasn't worth the trouble, if you ask me. But when I heard his name, I was afraid he had somehow learned I was here, had come to harass me or try and cause problems for Ben and me. I know it sounds irrational, but the part of me that knows him — knew him — *was* irrational. My relief was in knowing that no one could be abused by him again."

She began trembling. "Jeff, I was engaged to him. Can you believe that? I almost married Frank Hamilton." She said the name as if she were coughing up something vile.

Jeff put his arm around her shoulders. "But you didn't marry him. That's the important thing."

"Ben doesn't know about any of this, though — that I was engaged to someone else, someone who treated people like that, treated *me* like that." Her eyes were filled with pain when she looked at Jeff. "I suppose I'm going to have to tell him."

"I think you should. A lot of things are going to come out during the course of this investigation. Won't it be better if he hears about this from you? Before you tell the police?"

"Do you really think it will come out? I mean, that was so long ago."

Jeff was surprised that she thought six years was a long time. At her age, he supposed, it might seem that way. Or, perhaps, it had something to do with what life handed you in any given stretch. Everything's relative.

"Jennifer, I ran one simple check this afternoon and learned that both you and Frank had lived in Indianapolis at the same time."

"You're investigating? But —"

"Just taking a shortcut for Brookner, shaving off a little time. A good friend of mine is with the FBI. I offered to give him a call." Jeff finished off his drink. "My point is, it's relatively easy to get the surface information about a person, that first layer of existence. After that? Well, the detectives ask a lot of questions and start piecing together the puzzle.

"I have to report what I learned to Brookner," Jeff continued. "And I won't be surprised if he's already found out for himself."

"Does that mean you suspect *me?* I'm telling you the truth, Jeff. I did not kill Frank Hamilton."

Jeff wanted to believe her. And he had to admit, he did. For the most part. But he'd been surprised before. Heat-of-passion murders could be committed by damn near anyone. For now, though, he didn't want to scare her away. "I didn't run background checks until after Davenport was found. You knew him. That's why you were on the list. End of story."

"Why would they be checking if they think Edward committed suicide?" She set her glass down with a bang. "I'll bet they don't believe he killed himself any more than I do." After a moment, she added, "If it turns out he did, though, someone pushed him to it. Pushed him really hard."

"Do you know anyone who would want to? Push him, I mean?"

"No. Of course, why should anyone believe me? I've been lying to everyone. I told you I didn't know Frank. I repeated that story twice to Detective Brookner. And I haven't told my own husband any of it." By the time she'd finished talking, she was shaking.

Jeff pulled her closer. "You need to talk to Ben as soon as you can. After that, go tell Brookner what you've told me. Where is Ben, by the way?"

She looked at her watch. "He should be here any time now to change for dinner. I told him to meet me in the room if I didn't come back to the Parlor."

Jeff needed some time to assimilate everything he'd learned from Jennifer over the past several minutes. He steered the conversation in another direction. "Last night was *Breakfast at Tiffany's*, today, *Gatsby*. What do you two have in store for your fans tonight?"

She laughed. "We do get into the theme of things, don't we? Amazing, how film and literature dictate fashion."

"I think it's only the ones set in period." Jeff thought about Mel Littlefield's comparing him to Spacey in *L.A. Confidential*, that movie set in the fifties that was so much more appealing than the book. "I don't see much in contemporary movies that makes me want to get rid of the classics."

"I agree. But to answer your question: I'm not giving anything away. You'll just have to join us for dinner to see what we've come up with."

He accepted the invitation. He thought about making another drink, then decided against it for fear he'd disturb Trudy, whose even breathing indicated that she'd fallen asleep. He could feel Jennifer's breathing, too, seated beside him. She seemed calmer now that she'd admitted to her relationship with Frank Hamilton.

Jeff heard the sound of a key finding its mark in a door's lock. At first, he wasn't sure if it was the door to the suite, but then tumblers rattled and clicked into place, and Ben walked in.

Jeff didn't understand at first why Ben stopped in his tracks and glared at the love seat where Jeff was sitting with Jennifer. He watched as Ben's head jerked toward the bed.

Jeff's gaze followed. Trudy's tiny figure could barely be detected. To anyone not knowing she was there it looked like the bed was unoccupied . . . now. But it did look like it had been occupied recently.

Jeff suddenly, regretfully, realized what the scene must've looked like to Ben. He stood, hands outstretched, and started to explain.

Ben balled up his fists and lunged.

Chapter Twenty-one

Jeff felt as if he were in slow motion, trapped in a bubble of water, drifting while everything around him happened at triple speed. Although he hadn't been prepared for a confrontation, he had dodged just in time to avoid a broken nose. The blow ricocheted off his cheekbone just below his right eye.

Jeff staggered and found his balance. He gingerly touched the wound, then looked at his fingers. Blood. He looked at Ben's hand and saw the ring. Nice touch.

"Ben!" Jennifer bolted from the love seat. "What do you think you're doing?"

"The same thing any other man would do who'd just caught another man in his wife's bed. What the hell's going on here?"

"For God's sake! Shouldn't you have asked that question *before* you hit Jeff? You've never acted like this before."

"I've never found you in a hotel room with another man before."

"You still haven't," Jennifer said through gritted teeth.

The room grew quiet.

"I beg your pardon?" The corners of Jeff's

mouth twitched slightly. He fought hard to keep from grinning. He watched as Jennifer's expression changed from anger to realization to embarrassment.

"I —"

"You don't need to explain. If I were in Ben's shoes, I would probably react the same way."

"Benjamin Hurst," Jennifer said with the tone a mother would use on a child who'd been a bully. "Shouldn't you be apologizing to Jeff?"

"You heard him. He knows how it is."

"Your gender exasperates me," she said hotly. "I could write a book. You know what? Maybe I should. I'll call it *Women Are From Venus, Men Are From Hell*."

"I'll buy a copy." Trudy sat up in the bed.

Ben threw a confused look at the strange girl.

Jennifer went to her. "Trudy, we woke you. I'm so sorry."

"No, that's okay."

Jennifer gazed at her husband for a long time, then turned to Jeff. "Would you keep an eye on her?"

"Sure. It'll give us a chance to visit."

Jennifer took Ben's arm and led him toward the French doors that opened onto a deck. "I need to tell you about someone I once knew."

After they left, Jeff seated himself on the

edge of the bed beside Trudy.

"Are you okay?" she asked.

"It could've been a lot worse." He glanced at the couple on the deck, sitting across from one another, holding hands. He wondered how Ben would take the news of Jennifer's past. It was apparent Ben loved his wife. Hopefully, he loved her enough.

"Trudy?" Jeff suspected it would be difficult for the girl to talk, but he needed to learn what was going on. "Do you feel like talking about it?"

"I can try. My brother may have been unscrupulous, but I don't think someone should've killed him for it."

"He arranged for you to meet him here?"

She nodded. "He had an envelope messengered to me at the shop. In it was an airline ticket, a confirmation letter from the Murray Hotel for two nights, and three hundred dollars in traveler's checks."

"Do you know why he wanted you here?"

"Partly. He told me he'd worked out a way to get Mrs. Appleby's tea set, but he needed some help playing a trick on someone. He knew so much about it that I didn't have any reason to suspect anything. So I came here thinking I could somehow help get the tea set and take it back to her.

"But last night, when he came to my hotel, I found out he wasn't trying to get the tea set for Mrs. Appleby at all. Honestly, Mr.

Talbot, after I learned that, I told him I wasn't about to help him. Mrs. Appleby has been more like family to me than anyone else. I'd never do anything that would hurt her.

"I was trying to figure out what to do when you found me. But I wanted to see if I could talk some sense into Frank first." Trudy looked down. "Only he never showed up."

"Did you try to call him?"

"Yes. I left several messages. You can check with the front desk if you don't believe me."

"Trudy, I don't doubt that you're telling me the truth. I'm just trying to find out what happened to him. You want to know that, don't you?"

"Of course I do."

"Okay, try to remember: Did he tell you anything that might help?"

"No. At least I don't think so. All he said last night — other than to meet him — was that he'd found a way to make a lot more money on the tea set and he didn't care who ended up with it. He said he could make enough so that he'd never have to worry about money again."

"Do you know how he intended to do that?"

"He wouldn't say."

"Was someone else in on this with him?"

"He wouldn't tell me that, either. He just

said there was someone willing to pay a huge sum of money for the set."

"Was it Blanche?"

"No. I wondered that, too. But that's all he *would* tell me. It wasn't her."

Jeff said, more to himself than to Trudy, "I wonder if it was the woman I saw him talking to last night."

"You saw him with someone?"

He told her about the scene in the gardens, the woman — or, at least, he assumed it was a woman — in the picture hat, Frank's body language that revealed his frustration, his anger. When Jeff demonstrated by popping his forehead with his palm, the young woman flinched.

"Trudy, I'm sorry. I didn't mean to startle you." He gently touched her arm.

Suddenly, he wondered if Trudy trusted him. When he thought about it, he realized that they really didn't know each other very well. "I didn't kill your brother, Trudy. I hope you believe that."

"I'm sorry. I only jumped because you . . . I've seen Frank get angry more times than I care to remember. You reminded me of his cruel side when you did that. But I know you didn't kill him. Mrs. Appleby has told me several times that if I ever need anything when she's dead and gone, you're the one person I can truly rely on."

Jeff grinned. "I can't see her taking the

time to die, can you?"

"No." Trudy let out a little chuckle, then grew quiet. After a moment, she said, "Will you help me find out who killed him?"

"I'll do everything I can, Trudy. That's a promise." Jeff wondered how she'd summoned enough nerve to stand up to her bully brother. Likely, she was a lot stronger than she realized. Now she just needed to learn how to draw from that strength. "Trudy, you've heard of Edward Davenport, haven't you?"

"The auctioneer? Of course. Mrs. Appleby relies heavily on his writings when verifying English antiques. Why?"

"Do you know if your brother knew him?"

"Frank never mentioned him. But we haven't been in touch very much over the last couple of years. Usually just when Frank wanted help with one of his schemes."

"Davenport was supposed to conduct a special auction tomorrow — an auction that was to include the cabaret set." Jeff hated to upset Trudy further, but he charged ahead. "Trudy, this afternoon Davenport committed suicide."

"Suicide?" She was quiet for several moments. "But why would someone so passionate about antiques kill himself doing what he loved to do? And at a place where hundreds of antique lovers are gathered. Are you sure it was suicide?"

"Not completely, no. If it was murder, though, someone did a hell of a job making it look like suicide. The medical examiner is checking now for poisoning, signs of struggle, that sort of thing."

"Did he leave a note or anything to say why he'd do such a thing?"

"That's the big question. They didn't find one, and it makes me suspicious. I mean, Davenport was a writer. I can't imagine him checking out without some commentary. Yet, if someone killed him and made it look like a suicide — well, that took some doing. He was a big man.

"Hopefully, the ME's report will tell us something. Either way, I can't help but feel it's somehow tied to Frank's death."

The doors leading to the deck opened, and Jennifer and Ben walked arm in arm into the room. Although their eyes were rimmed red from what had to have been an emotional session, Jeff could see that they'd come through intact. Instinctively, he touched his own eye and winced. At least women could hide behind makeup. He was wondering if he'd have to resort to a pair of glasses when Jennifer walked over and gave him a hug. "It looks sexy," she whispered. "I wouldn't do a thing to cover it up, if I were you."

"A man's thoughts are never sacred when there's a woman in the room, are they?"

"You got that right," Ben said. "Jeff, I —"

"No need, Ben. I would've done the same thing." Jeff turned back to Trudy. "Would you like to join us for dinner tonight?"

"Thanks, Mr. Talbot, but this place is a little too fancy for me. I think I'll go downtown and get a sandwich."

Jennifer stepped in. "Trudy, are you sure? Because, if you need a dress, I've got —"

"Really, Jen. I appreciate it, but I'd rather not be around here tonight. You understand?"

Jennifer nodded.

Jeff understood, too. Trudy didn't want to be reminded of her brother. "Let me take you downstairs and get you a cab."

"No, thanks." Trudy got out of bed and slipped on her shoes. "I'll walk. It's only about fifteen minutes."

"I'm going to win this one, Trudy, so you might as well save us all some time."

Trudy obviously sensed Jeff's determination. She nodded and walked with him toward the door. Before leaving, Jeff said to the Hursts, "I'll see you at dinner."

Chapter Twenty-two

The phone's message light was flashing when Jeff entered his room.

Two new messages, the recording told him. The first was from Gordy.

"Sorry, bud. All hell's broke loose, and I'm on my way to Chicago. Stay out of jail."

Jeff punched seven, and the system moved to the second message.

Sheila's voice, excited, announced that she had news and asked that he call as soon as he could.

Jeff wondered why women couldn't just leave a message. They always wanted to watch your face when they delivered news, capture your reaction. Second best was delivering news over the phone. They'd do it if they had no other choice, but they'd be damned if they were going to leave a recorded message and miss your reaction altogether.

He called.

"Where have you been?" Sheila's voice was high-pitched, a phenomenon that rarely occurred. It put Jeff's nerves on edge. "I hit paydirt, and you're nowhere to be found!"

"Sheila, honey, calm down. You're not the only one who's been working." An attempt at explaining the altercation with Ben Hurst could wait until later.

"Oh. Sorry. Well, don't you want to know what I found out?"

He had an image of her expression, the anxiousness to be a part of things, the excitement at being able to help. "Should I write this down?"

"Jeffrey."

When she used his full name, he knew he'd better cut the crap. "Yes, ma'am. Pen in hand."

She cleared her throat. "The document you have is a diploma given to Eric Von Screibtisch by Friedrich Wilhelm University in Berlin. He graduated with a doctorate in *Europaervolkswirtschaft*. That's the phrase you gave me. Roughly translated, it means European socioeconomics. He was married, had one daughter, taught at his alma mater — or whatever they call it in Germany — for fifteen years before retiring."

"Retiring? If he did all this over the normal course of things, then he would've been — what? — thirty-seven, thirty-eight? Same age as I am now. Hell, I can't imagine *retiring*."

"But you did retire, basically. You left the FBI so you could get into antiques."

"I don't think of it that way. *Retired* is synonymous with *old* in my book."

211

"Are you still stewing over Frank Hamilton's 'old man' remark?"

"No, that's not it." Jeff asked himself if that *was* it. Was he really that sensitive about his age? He didn't think so. "No," he repeated with more conviction. "Retirement is my grandfather shuffling around the house with Auntie Pim taking care of him."

"Need I remind you, Mr. Talbot," Sheila said, "that when I agreed to marry you, you assured me you'd never grow old?"

People always said that a notable age difference between partners didn't matter as the couple grew older together. Jeff was finding the opposite to be true. When he was younger, he could keep up with Sheila's boundless energy. Lately, he'd felt a turning point approaching, and that damned climb to the fort had hammered it home.

For now, though, he needed to get the conversation back on track before resorting to words like *Little Missy* and *Young Lady*.

"Maybe the German translation for *retired* is the same as *resigned*. Did you find out anything about whether Screibtisch moved on to another university or to some other academic field?"

"No. At least, not so far. It's as if he dropped off the face of the earth. The trail stops with his resignation."

"What about the wife and daughter?"

"Fortunately, I have a friend from a chat

room on European cooking. She knows some German and gave me the gist of a newspaper article I found — something about Screibtisch receiving some sort of recognition. She said the article reported that Screibtisch's wife, Ilka, and daughter, Ingrid, attended a ceremony in his honor."

"Where are they now?"

"Good question. I can't find anything about any of them after he left the university."

"Damn it. All three of them couldn't have just evaporated." Even as he said it, Jeff realized how ridiculous it sounded.

"Stranger things have happened. I'll dig some more." Sheila paused. "It's after six there. Wish I could see you all decked out for the evening."

"You and me both. I haven't had a chance to change."

"We'd better get off the phone, then. I'll call you tonight if I get any more information."

The two said their good-byes, then Jeff began dressing. He wondered absently what the Hursts would be wearing and decided that their effect was probably never as striking and powerful when each was alone.

He buttoned his white Burberry and set about threading a cuff link shank through one of the sleeves. The links were a Napoleonic design, gold with a rich carnelian ground. Surmounted on each red disk was a golden bee. He had purchased them during a Napoleonic costume exhibit in New York at about the same time he'd begun searching for Blanche's cabaret set.

The strange and deadly events of the last twenty-four hours made him question his prior premonitory actions: attempting to book the Napoleon Suite — and feeling unlucky upon learning that it was already spoken for, buying the cuff links, studying up on Napoleon and Josephine. Of course, the research gave him a base knowledge of Empire antiques, which had proven lucrative many times over. Now, though, as he looked at the cuff links, he saw a red flag waving an announcement to everyone at the festival: "Here I am, anxiously waiting to drop a fortune on a tea set." His lips tightened. He contemplated wearing a different pair but didn't want to waste any more time.

As he aggressively threaded the second cuff, he went over what he'd learned so far. Everyone — Ben and Jennifer Hurst, Lily Chastain, Ruth Ann Longan, and Asia Graham (the Three Musketeers, as Gordy had cleverly called them), Frank Hamilton, Edward Davenport — either knew or had met everyone else before this year's festival.

He was still amazed at, and a little suspicious of, the coincidence of Jennifer Hurst's engagement to Frank Hamilton. Then, to top off everything, Trudy Blessing had turned out to be Hamilton's sister.

It suddenly occurred to Jeff that Trudy and Frank didn't share the same last name. Now, what the hell was that about? Could Trudy actually be married? Surely to God he'd know about *that*, wouldn't he? Just as surely, he questioned why he would. Until this afternoon, he and Trudy had never had a real conversation.

He wondered whether Trudy had called Blanche and told her about Frank's death, revealed that they were brother and sister. He would call Blanche before turning in tonight. With the time difference, he could catch her right after her dinner hour.

And the Three Musketeers. Did the three Southern women, like Athos, Porthos, and Aramis, have an all-for-one-and-one-for-all pact? If so, were they hiding something? Covering for one another? In on it together? In on what? Murder? Jeff shook his head, as if to erase the silly notion from his thoughts. Hell, with their obvious arthritis, osteoporosis, and canes, all three added together couldn't get the lid off a mayonnaise jar without the aid of a rubber grip and the local fire department.

A two-headed monster assaulted Jeff's conscience. It was created from Auntie Pim and Blanche, and both heads were talking at once but delivering a single message: Don't dismiss us just because we're *old*.

They were right. Two people were dead, and he couldn't rule out anyone as suspect.

He knotted his dark red silk tie, then studied his handiwork in the mirror. A vision of Davenport swinging from the balcony came to him, and he wedged his index finger between the shirt's top button and his neck and tugged slightly.

The auctioneer's suicide had something to do with Hamilton's murder, Jeff knew it. Both were here for the antique festival, and both were dead. Davenport was to conduct an auction that would include the cabaret set. Hamilton, Jeff had learned from Trudy, had meant to procure it, probably at any cost.

Maybe Hamilton and Davenport didn't know each other. Jeff had assumed they did, but hundreds of people attended this event each year. It was just as likely that the two had never actually met. If Hamilton had known Davenport at all, it may have been in the same way Jeff did, by reading the auctioneer's articles in the trade magazines.

Jeff suspected that Hamilton himself had hidden the German document in the Raviro clock. At the same time, he had to admit that it might just be a coincidence, that the document might have nothing to do with the two dead men. The information Sheila had given him was interesting, but it didn't prove anything.

Hell, he thought, that document might

have been stowed away in the little piano for years, its value — if it had any collectible value — deteriorating with exposure to metal and air and silverfish. It may very well have been inside the piano when the antique clock was acquired by the hotel. Jeff, who had always taken a certain pride in locating hidden passageways and secret compartments, had only stumbled upon the hinged piano lid after giving up his search of everything else.

Jeff put on his black suit coat and slid his wallet into the breast pocket. From the nightstand he took two folded sheets of paper — the German document and his notes from the conversations with Sheila and Gordy — and slipped them behind the wallet.

Many developments had transpired since he'd last spoken with the detective in charge of the case — or cases, now that two people were dead. Jeff needed to track Brookner down before joining the Hursts for dinner. He took one last look at himself in the mirror.

"Not too shabby," he said to his reflection, "as long as I don't stand next to Ben Hurst."

Hurst. Jeff had almost forgotten the punch. He leaned in and examined his cheek.

The flesh was chafed red, but the scratch was no more than an inch long. Since everyone would be dressed to the nines, his injury probably wouldn't even be noticed.

He grabbed his key and hurried out the door.

Chapter Twenty-three

When no one answered Jeff's knock on the interrogation room door, he tried the knob and found it was unlocked. He opened it a few inches and glanced inside. A strip of light from the hallway's overhead fixture stretched diagonally across a bare desk. Jeff swung the door open. Now he could see that a telephone was on the desk's far corner, but everything he'd seen there earlier — file folders, fax sheets, coffee mugs, half-eaten doughnuts, photos, maps — was gone. The room smelled of furniture polish and looked as if it had been vacant for years.

An odd sensation washed over him, as if he'd dreamed the day's bizarre chain of events during a disjointed sleep brought on by jet lag and stress.

He pulled the door shut and had started back down the hall, trying to decide what to do next, when Mel Littlefield rounded the corner.

She saw him and let out a whoop: fitting, considering her Indian ancestry. "Spacey has his work cut out for him tonight."

"Thanks, Officer." His response was a little

too exuberant. He laid the blame more on the reassurance that he wasn't trapped in a nightmare than on the compliment.

"What happened in there?" He nodded toward the office.

"Never mind that. What happened to your eye?"

Jeff missed a beat. "I had a run-in with a clothes hanger."

"Yeah? What was her name?"

Jeff ignored the question. "Your interrogation room looks like my desk used to when I'd sewn up a case. I couldn't wait to box it all up and be rid of it."

"Not the case here — sewing it up, I mean. The boss was talking about getting away from here for a while. Couldn't just leave everything, so I took it all downtown to the chief's office."

"You haven't seen Brookner, have you?"

"The boss? Just left him out front."

Jeff turned to go.

"Watch out for those fancy hangers, Mr. Talbot. They'll get you every time."

He exited the hotel on the Parlor level and descended the red-carpeted steps. Clouds overhead had darkened since he was last outside. The wind whipped and snapped the row of flags along the front porch, like wash on a line. Brookner had his back to him and was leaning over the wrought-iron fence that separated the sidewalk from the Tea Garden below.

"Brookner!" Jeff was glad to see the crusty detective, further proof that he wasn't losing his mind. He pulled the two pieces of paper from his pocket and the wind tried to snatch them from his hand. He tightened his grip. "I'll bet a bottle of whiskey against that steak you're looking forward to that I've turned up more than you have today."

"Steak? Oh, right." Brookner eked one more draw out of a cigarette, then squashed it on the sidewalk and kicked it into the flower bed. "No steak on my menu tonight. I'll take that bet, though. I've learned a thing or — what the hell?" He examined Jeff's cheek. "You're the one needs a steak."

"It's not that bad."

"What happened?"

He hesitated. "I caught a stray buggy whip."

"Yep, that's exactly what I would've guessed. Get five or six of those a week. Real common." He stared at Jeff a minute. "Care to try again?"

Jeff was debating his comeback when a kid plodded up the sidewalk grumbling to himself. He looked to be about fifteen and was dressed like a real working cowboy from the waist down: both jeans and boots were well-worn and as dusty as Oklahoma in '32. Waist up, he had on a Mackinac Island T-shirt that had also been a party to the Dust Bowl and listed the top ten lies a Mackinac Islander will tell you — the only one Jeff could make out under the dirt was You'll Get Used to the Smell — and a cap with painted-on seagull droppings.

"Shawn McGuire, is that you?" Brookner fought a grin as he spoke. "Damn me, but I don't reckon I've ever seen you on foot. Somebody steal all your horses?"

Shawn stopped. "Same as. Some damn fool we rented to didn't pay attention to the sign telling amateurs to stay off the cliff road. Got spooked, *naturally*, and parked Dan and Pat and my best buggy in Haskell's yard." The boy looked toward the cliff beyond the Grand. "Storm's coming, too, which will only make it worse. Pat's so damn curious she might decide to take a gander at what's over that ledge before I get there." Shawn nodded to the men and started trotting up the hill.

"Hang on there, Shawn." Brookner looked at Jeff. "You been on a carriage ride yet?"

Jeff shook his head.

Brookner turned back to the boy. "I'll get it for you if you can give me an hour or so before you need it back."

Shawn shrugged. "Sounds good to me. I gotta go tend to the others and check harness for tomorrow's boatloads of greenhorns. Bring 'em to the house when you're through and I'll put them to bed." Shawn turned and went back down the hill.

Brookner started walking. Jeff followed.

It was a steep climb. Brookner didn't talk, thank God. Jeff wasn't sure if he could match the detective's pace and carry on a conversation. A string of Victorian mansions faced the Straits. At the top, Brookner told him that most were summer homes.

Jeff took in the view while Brookner expertly backed the team and carriage, then turned them onto the narrow road that led back down to the hotel.

"You've done this before." Jeff hoisted himself onto the seat next to Brookner. Suddenly he felt silly in his French cuffs and patent leather shoes.

Brookner held the reins tight while they made their way down the steep hill. "I worked summers up here when I was Shawn's age, driving delivery wagons. Covered every square inch of this island."

After they'd made it down below the hotel's property, Brookner reined the team into a right turn and took the same route Jeff had walked earlier along the boardwalk. "Being a guest of the Grand probably means you haven't eaten at any of the downtown establishments."

Jeff wasn't sure why, but he felt defensive. Although staying at the Grand gave a feeling of eliteness, he'd found it was interpreted as snobbishness by some. "Actually, I had lunch today at the fort."

"Doesn't count. It's run by the Grand."

"Come on. You're telling me the fort's run by the Grand Hotel?"

"Not the fort. The restaurant."

"It's called a tea room."

"I stand corrected."

Jeff laughed. "I didn't realize I sounded like such a fussy ass."

Brookner waved him off. "All depends on the kind of company you keep, I suppose. Do you appreciate good barbecue?"

"Hell, yes."

Brookner looked at his clothes. "Afraid you'll mess up your fancy duds?"

"We have dry cleaners in Seattle."

"Hang on, then. You're in for a treat." Brookner expertly worked the team and buggy around small knots of tourists and cabs picking up groups of people in garb similar to Jeff's. The detective used several choice curse words, obviously irritated with pedestrians who seemed oblivious to traffic. "I wonder if they think they can't get run over by horses? Damned fools."

"Maybe you can explain something. When I was driving the rental from Pellston Airport, I saw three different designs on Michigan's license tags. What do you do, give your inmates multiple choice?"

"Looks that way, doesn't it? Bottom line is revenue. The old secretary of state saw no

223

reason to change the tags when a lot of other states were going with fancier ones. Said the blue and white was just fine.

"Then we got a new secretary — a female. I don't know where that car idea came from; you have to be standing over it with a magnifying glass to tell what the hell it is. About a dozen rear-end collisions got blamed on it — people getting too close tryin' to make it out. Anyhow, then we got the one with the bridge at sunset. Now we got construction everywhere you take a mind to drive. Revenue."

"What about the two pronunciations of Mackinac? I know it's the French spelling, but I keep hearing people say both 'Mackinaw' and 'Mackinak.' "

"That's because they're idiots. It's all 'Mackinaw.' And before you ask, we're Michiganians, not Michiganders. It was less of a problem before the state legislature officially announced that we're Michiganians."

"It all sounds like a conspiracy theory to confuse out-of-staters."

"Wouldn't surprise me."

"I doubt much would surprise you."

"You got that right."

They followed the street along the harbor, and it wasn't long till Jeff could smell the spicy sweet aroma of sauce and hickory. "What's a barbecue joint doing down here?"

"Not even a joint, actually. Guy by the name of Brian cooks it in front of his mother's bed-and-breakfast. Usually just for lunch, but he's cooking for a fund-raiser to-night."

"Fund-raiser?"

"Yep. A gal in the city offices just had cancer surgery. The true islanders — the folks who stay here year round — are a close-knit group. Have to be when you live isolated like they do."

Brookner pulled the team to a stop. Jeff pulled a bill from his wallet and handed it to Brookner.

"Shit, Talbot. Barbecue don't cost fifty bucks, even on Mackinac Island."

"I like to help out when I can."

Chapter Twenty-four

Brookner returned, carrying a large brown paper bag with grease stains freckling the sides and a couple of cans of pop stacked end to end. He set the items in the buggy's floor, then climbed to his seat and unpacked the goods. A sizeable wad of paper napkins went to Jeff, followed by a Styrofoam container with a plastic fork handle sticking through the lid. Next, he handed Jeff a can of pop. When he snapped the lid off a twin to Jeff's Styrofoam bowl and started eating potato salad, Jeff followed suit.

Brookner said something to the team, and the horses started down the street. Jeff wasn't aware that you could put horses on autopilot. The two men ate and talked small talk while the horses pulled the buggy down the street. This area was very different from the bustle of downtown. Bed-and-breakfasts were to the left, with guests gathered in white wicker on front porches. On the right were places that reminded him of the fishing cabins along the lakes where he fished with Gordy.

When they'd finished the potato salad, Brookner reached in the bag again and pulled out two enormous disks wrapped in white butcher paper. He handed one to Jeff, then unwrapped the other and aproned the white paper around the sandwich. *When in Rome,* Jeff thought, and once again mimicked the detective's approach.

Brookner took a bite, groaned something as near to orgasmic as Jeff cared to hear from any man, then continued eating in silence. Jeff wondered whether the detective was exercising a long-established habit of not talking business over meals or whether the barbecue was really that good. Either, Jeff decided, was acceptable.

He took a bite. His eighty-dollar shirt didn't matter anymore. He'd buy another one if he had to. This was the best barbecue, the tenderest pulled beef he'd ever had. He felt like he was somehow cheating on his chef-wife.

"Okay, Talbot." Brookner sucked barbecue sauce from his fingers, then wadded the white butcher paper and deposited it in the brown bag between his feet. "Tell me what you got."

Jeff hadn't finished his sandwich, but he was on the detective's turf. He did as he was told. He reported the background information Gordy Easthope had gathered on the Hursts, Hamilton, Davenport, and the three old ladies. He told about the surprise run-in with Trudy Blessing, and how he'd learned that she was Hamilton's sister. He added the news about Jennifer Hurst's engagement to Hamilton. He finished up with the document he'd found in Hamilton's suite, and what Sheila had learned about it over the Internet.

Brookner was visibly surprised. "I'd like to know how in the hell you got the feds to co-operate so easily. God knows I never seem to have much luck with them."

"I'm helping you, aren't I?"

"Oh, yeah. I guess you do still fit the slot. At least you're not belligerent like some of the other G-men I've dealt with. Antiques must've softened you some." Brookner chewed at some sauce near the corner of his mustache. "Either that, or you miss sitting in an office making phone calls till your ass goes numb."

Jeff remembered how he'd felt earlier, being stuck in his room making calls. The same fate awaited him again tonight. "No, I don't miss that part of it. But it does feel good to look for the missing pieces. Of course, the document might not have anything to do with the cases. It may have been in that clock for years."

"Damned coincidences. Do nothin' but muddy up an investigation. I'll have to talk to the Hurst woman again and hunt down the sister." Brookner lit a cigarette. "Ever have barbecue that good?"

Personally, Jeff wouldn't have covered the

taste with nicotine. But he said, "I have to hand it to you, Detective. Definitely worth missing a meal at the Grand for."

Brookner nodded, apparently satisfied.

"Report came back from Nic." He relaced the reins through his fingers and popped them against the horses' rumps. One whinnied its disagreement, but stepped lively nonetheless, and the team quickly settled into a trot. "Like you figured, Hamilton died shortly after midnight. Had been in the rain — and the fountain — for several hours. Which, as we both know, plays hell with evidence. Still yet, the lab up in Marquette is testing the lug wrench, although I doubt they'll find anything after that much time in the water. But you never know. It could still have some hair samples and matter stuck to it. Enough was missing from the victim, that's for sure."

"Anything on Davenport?"

"Death by strangulation. Surprise, surprise," he said. "Nothing that shows any foul play," he added, replacing the sarcasm with weariness.

"Have you been able to learn whether he has any family?"

"No family. At least, according to his housekeeper there isn't anyone. I called his residence in New York. I was leaving a message on his answering machine. Housekeeper picked up as soon as I said I was a detective.

Told me she comes in a couple days a week to clean and cook up a few meals. Also told me that Davenport didn't have a wife or any relatives. Said the only things he gets in the mail besides bills are antique magazines and official-looking stuff — number ten envelopes with business logos printed on them. When I told her he was dead, she said, 'Guess I'll be takin' these casseroles home with me. He sure won't be a-needin' them.' " Brookner laughed one of those laughs that tells you he's heard it all and appreciates a practical mind.

The wind stopped suddenly. Jeff was about to comment on what that meant in Seattle when Brookner looked at the sky, then turned the team down a side street and circled the block. "With any luck," he said, heading west down Main, "we'll get back to the Grand before the cloudburst."

"Have you turned up anything else?"

"The housekeeper — the one at the hotel who found Davenport — is pretty shook up, but she seems to recall somebody standing in the hallway when she ran for help. She says she ran for help," Brookner added. "I say she just plain ran. Superstitious or something. I've never seen anyone more afraid to talk about something."

"Did she remember anything about who she saw?"

"Said it was a white person. Really narrows

it down, doesn't it? Anyway, I interviewed the grounds crew, too. Everybody showed up for work like they were supposed to today. Same crew as yesterday. Nobody quit or called in sick.

"I need *something*, Talbot. It's been forty years since the last murder on Mackinac Island. That one was never solved. If this one isn't solved either, we'll never live it down. Media pounces on this sort of thing. Always has, but its reach is a hell of a lot farther now."

"Do you think the two deaths are related?"

"Sure as hell do. Murder just doesn't happen here. With that in mind, what are the odds of two deaths from unnatural causes happening at the same event, hours apart, *not* being related?"

"Too much of a spread for my wallet."

"We need a suicide note or a skeleton in a closet or something on Davenport."

The rain started sporadically, with drops the size of quarters falling onto the horses' rumps and forming mud spots in their dusty coats. It broke loose then, and in less time than it takes to tell it, both man and beast were soaked. Brookner urged the horses on, rushing through downtown as Jeff watched people scramble to get out of the way. Many of the pedestrians were in a state of panic, darting this way and that across the street, zigzagging in order not to be run down by wagons and bicyclists. Several drenched people tried to hail the horse-drawn taxis.

The scene was not unlike Manhattan in sudden downpours that send pedestrians scrambling for cabs. Although there were far less people on this island, there were even fewer drivers for hire by comparison. One might argue, however, that these four-legged throwbacks to another time moved a little faster than the cabs in the Big Apple.

Thunder crashed, and Dan and Pat reared as if a string of firecrackers had been thrown at their flanks. Brookner maintained control, expertly working the reins. He turned the team up Hoban Street and reined them in at Market. "We're already soaked. If you don't mind walking, I'll take the rig over to Shawn. I don't know that restaging what you saw will do any good, but nothing else is, either. I'll meet you up top in about thirty."

Jeff hopped down and started toward Grand Avenue.

"You don't have any qualms about being stranded on an island with a murderer, do you?"

Brookner's question stopped Jeff in his tracks. He hadn't thought of it that way before. "No, but I'm not sure why."

"I'll tell you why. You've gotten to know several of those people relatively quickly." He nodded toward the Grand's hill when he spoke. "They appear to be normal, up-standing citizens. Some might even say trust-worthy folks. You don't want to suspect any of them. You've gone through some motions of playing cop, used your training — what little is left of it — to get some facts a little quicker than I could've gotten them. Remember this: at least one of 'em has let himself — or herself, if you wanna get PC — get caught up in what looks like a crime of passion."

"You're wrong, Brookner. My approach is just different from yours. Did you ever stop to think that we've covered quite a bit of ground in a short amount of time? We both know that's the key to any investigation: Get as much as you can the first twenty-four hours. It will work to our advantage that we take very different approaches, like good-cop-bad-cop. Every damn one of those people is on my list."

"Good for you, Talbot. You've got a list. But yours isn't necessarily a *suspect* list. That's *all* my list is: suspects. The sister, the ex-fiancé, her husband, even your Three Musketeers and the dead auctioneer. Especially the auctioneer. They're all suspects. And they're all on my list."

A stream of water ran down Jeff's forehead from his rain-soaked hair. Droplets beaded, clung to his lashes. He blinked rapidly. "Am I on that list?"

Brookner waited a beat before he spoke. "No."

"Why not?"

"You wanna be?" he asked sarcastically.

"Come on. You know what I mean."

Brookner's gaze was steady. "I've been a cop for most of my life. Call it a gut instinct if you want to. Add to it this: Why would you come all the way out here to kill him? You'd have a helluva lot better chance getting away with it in Seattle."

Brookner snapped the reins and was gone.

Jeff had to give the guy credit. When he wanted to put things back on a business level, he didn't jack around. And he'd shaken Jeff up with the island remark, too.

Islands. Jeff had stayed on islands before, but never one this small. He walked up the hill toward his hotel. The day had been hot and humid. Now, the cool rain clashed with the heat held by the ground and formed large, steamy fog pockets that settled over the Tea Garden.

Anxiety came over Jeff. As the fog thickened, he felt something tighten around his chest like a vise. He bounded up the wide staircase and ran to the west end of the hotel's long porch. He strained to see the lights of the mainland. Nothing. He tried to see the lights strung along the lines of Mackinac Bridge, those he'd seen last night that put him in mind of a skeleton, the brittle bones of its form. Again, nothing. Panic gripped him. His heart beat faster. He took a deep breath, told himself to shake it off, shake away the fear of being trapped on the island. A chilling glimpse of life in Sheila's world came over him. He'd never felt more isolated.

Chapter Twenty-five

He thought he could get through the Parlor without being noticed. Quite a few people were having after-dinner drinks, and he hoped they were interested enough in one another not to notice him walking through, dripping all over the carpet of geraniums. This was the second night he had missed out on the after-dinner drinks.

"Jeff!" It was Jennifer Hurst's voice.

Hearing her reminded him that he'd forgotten about his dinner date with her and Ben. He turned. "I'm —"

"Jeff, what on earth?" Jennifer rushed to him, followed closely by Ben. "It's cliché, but I have to say it. You look like you've seen a ghost!"

"What?"

"You're positively white." Jennifer grabbed his arm, then drew away and gave her now wet hand a confused look. "And your . . . your arm's wet."

"For all your observations, my dear wife, you missed the obvious. He's dripping." Ben pulled a crisply folded handkerchief from his back pocket and handed it to Jeff. "You're going to need a hell of a lot more than this, but it's a start."

Jeff accepted it and sluiced water from his face, then looked at the couple. Jennifer was wearing a shimmering white gown covered with hundreds of ostrich feathers. Ben was in full dress, right down to the white tie, tails, top hat, and cane.

Just as he suspected, he would have faded into the background had he been with them all evening. Although that would've been preferable to the stares he was now getting.

"Do you dance like Fred and Ginger, too?"

The Hursts groaned.

"You've heard that line a time or two tonight."

Ben said, "A time or two."

"I know we seem a little over the top," Jennifer said, "but you'll appreciate it once you know the facts. Ben's hat and cane are authentic. They were Astaire's in *Top Hat*."

Jeff's brows shot up. "You're right, I do. But your dress?" He knew for a fact that Ginger Rogers had been only a little over five feet.

"Oh, I own the dress from the movie as well. But I found this copy last year in New York at a vintage fashion show."

"My apologies for assuming otherwise." Jeff bowed slightly. "Actually, I should be apologizing about dinner. Brookner grabbed me to go downtown, and I didn't have a chance to let you know."

"Never mind that. Are you okay?"

"Nothing a hot shower and a gallon of coffee won't fix."

"What did the detective do? Throw you in the lake?"

"He probably wanted to." Jeff handed the now soaking wet handkerchief back to Ben. "I suppose I should get out of these clothes."

Jennifer said, "You'll be back down, won't you?"

"Sure. Out, anyway. I have to meet Brookner in the Cupola in a little while."

"So do we," Ben said. "He wants us to help re-create what you saw last night."

"I hope it does some good."

"Oh," Jennifer said, "the concierge was looking for you, something about a message."

"Thanks. I'll check at his desk on my way up."

"We'll see you in the Cupola, then."

The leather inlays of the oak partners' desk that served as the concierge station had been recently replaced and retooled with finely detailed borders in gold. The decision to alter such an antique would be a difficult call and Jeff wondered how furniture gurus Leigh and Leslie Keno might react if they saw it. Their mantra, "Don't Refinish," held merit and was proved widely in the American antiques world as sound advice. Jeff usually agreed, knowing that to defy it meant a hefty markdown in value. But antiques pressed into constant service would require attention, just as they might have a hundred years ago.

Slumped in a leather chair behind the desk was a blond-haired boy in his teens wearing a red blazer and a sullen smirk. He made no move to sit up when Jeff approached.

"I understand you're holding a message for me."

"Depends on who you are."

Jeff's jaw tightened. He hadn't cut a four-figure check to be treated like this by the help. "I hope to God you're not going to tell me you're the concierge. Is he around?"

"The concierge has left for the evening."

"Then the concierge can expect a letter from me about your lack of people skills."

He shrugged, his acne-scarred face showing no emotion. "I'll be gone by the time he receives it."

Jeff wondered what school district the little prick lived in. Shouldn't he have been back in class two weeks ago, advertising Hilfiger clothes and snapping girls' bras? "Must be nice not to need this job next year."

That got his attention. He moved to the edge of the seat. "Sorry, sir. Your name?"

Jeff gave it to him.

The kid handed him an envelope and a question. "You're not gonna write that letter, are you?"

Jeff didn't give him the satisfaction of a response.

He took the stairs beside the concierge station, ripping open the envelope as he went. He unfolded the note and looked at the three words: Call your wife.

That was it? Why hadn't she just left a message on voice mail?

In his room, he peeled the wet clothes from his shivering body and dropped them in the tub, then wrapped himself in the hotel's robe and dialed his home number. After four rings, voice mail on that end kicked in, and he told his own voice that he'd be in the room till midnight.

A pot of coffee was what he needed. He put one on to brew, then called housekeeping to pick up his suit and do what they could for it. After the maid left, he downed a full mug of the hot liquid just as fast as his body would let him.

The second mug wasn't as urgent. He took it onto the balcony. The rain had stopped, and he searched for the Mackinac Bridge. Its lights, like tiny, flickering white Christmas bulbs, winked reassuringly in the distance. The structure no longer looked skeletal. He heaved a sigh of relief, as if the bridge were his only link to civilization.

He went back inside, checked the clock on the nightstand, which read 9:57, and flipped on the television. An *Antiques Roadshow* special, complete with behind-the-scenes footage, was about to begin. It was the best luck he'd had all day, so he settled against propped-up bed pillows to fill the minutes till midnight.

As the credits rolled two hours later, Jeff quickly dressed in a fresh shirt with the slacks and jacket he'd worn that afternoon. The message light was flashing, and he was amazed he hadn't noticed it earlier. Then he realized that Sheila must've been leaving him a message while he was trying to call her.

Phone tag, you're it, the blinking seemed to say. He'd have to call her after the meeting with Brookner.

The striped awning that formed a circus big top in the Cupola Bar couldn't have been more fitting for the scene unfolding when Jeff arrived.

In one ring was Brookner — he'd changed clothes as well — with Lieutenant Mel Littlefield and another cop Jeff hadn't met. The detective, one knee on the padded bench seat that bordered the room, was leaning over and pointing down toward the gardens. He held a walkie-talkie in his other hand.

In the middle ring were Ben and Jennifer Hurst, wearing the clothes they'd had on when Jeff first met them: Ben in a charcoal suit and Jennifer in the black dress, gloves, and picture hat.

Completing the three-ring circus was a group that included Lily Chastain, Asia Graham, and Ruth Ann Longan. There was no elevator to the Cupola, and Jeff wondered how the three had ever managed the stairs. He also wondered why.

Asia was seated in one of two wrought-iron chairs, drumming her fingers on the Frisbee-sized cocktail table. Ruth Ann was dragging a third chair over while Lily maneuvered herself into the seat next to Asia.

Jeff hurried over and rescued Ruth Ann.

"Why thank you, dear." She turned to him with a grateful smile and gasped when she saw his face. "You've been hurt!"

Asia craned her neck to see what the fuss was about, then announced, "You're lucky you didn't lose an eye."

"Asia's right," Lily said. "What happened?"

"You'll never believe it. I was downtown when the storm hit and there was a maiden in distress in a runaway carriage and —"

"Fine, then," snapped Asia. "Don't tell us."

Ruth Ann looked anxiously at him like she wanted to hear how the adventure had ended.

Lily grinned. "Now, Asia, be nice to the boy. He's only having a little fun."

Asia ignored her. "We heard there was something special going on up here tonight. Do you know what it's about?"

"I don't know that I'd call it special. The —"

"Isn't it a special program or something?" Ruth Ann asked.

There had been a pianist the night before. Jeff checked his watch, then pointed out the piano. "Someone will probably start playing in fifteen minutes or so."

"That'll just make it hard for us to hear one another." Asia started to get up.

"We can at least stay and order a drink," offered Lily.

"You can if you want to, but this old gal's turnin' in."

"Asia's right, Lily." Ruth Ann stood. "Tomorrow's going to be a long day."

"Nothin' but a bunch of party poopers." Lily struggled to her feet as she said it and followed the others toward the stairs.

Several people were in the bar now, sipping cocktails and whispering among themselves. None of them seemed curious about the police being there. A body could drop right in front of some people and they'd simply step over it on their way out.

Brookner turned and cursed when he saw the crowd that had gathered. He rapped a table three times with the walkie-talkie, but it didn't get the attention of the crowd. The noise continued.

Jeff expected a boisterous *Ladies and Gentlemen!* to come from the detective's lungs, closely followed by a buxom woman in sequins leading a trunk-to-tail string of elephants.

"What is this?" Brookner yelled. "A three-ring circus?"

The barmaid Jeff had talked with the night before walked past Brookner about then and said, "Helluva fine job of detecting." She pointed at the circus ceiling with one of her geranium-lacquered nails.

Brookner's glare followed the nail and he offered up a few choice words.

"People, let me have your attention." Brookner's voice held none of the pomp and circumstance of a ringmaster. The bubble was broken, and the detective got down to business.

"Mr. and Mrs. Hurst," Brookner said. "If you will go down to the garden, please, I have a couple of officers waiting there for you. They'll position you when I give them the word."

Brookner waited for the couple to leave.

"Talbot, I want you over here at the window."

Jeff walked over and stood beside the detective.

"You're sure you remember where you saw Hamilton last night?"

Jeff assured him that he did.

"Anything new from your contacts?"

He told the detective about the phone tag with Sheila. "I'll try her again when we're through here."

Brookner's walkie-talkie squawked.

"Yeah?"

"They're down here. Where do you want them?"

Brookner handed the walkie-talkie to Jeff.

He leaned over and looked down at the small group. Four faces were looking up at him. "For starters, have Ben and Jennifer look at each other, not up here."

The cop turned to the couple and spoke. Their heads went down.

"There. Now, she needs to step to the right. Good. Now, tell him to back up a couple steps." Jeff closed his eyes, summoned the image of Frank Hamilton and the mystery woman from the night before. He opened his eyes, peered back down at the two now standing in their places. He continued with the orchestration until the scene below him matched up with his memory.

Brookner looked at Jeff, then down at the scene. "You were right. Can't recognize them without the body language."

"Something's not right."

"Like what? Aren't they in the right places?"

"Yes, but something's missing." Jeff thought about it a minute. "There was a glint of light beside the woman last night. From up here, I thought maybe it was a Malibu light — you know, those lanterns that are close to the ground to highlight an area." Jeff radioed the cops and asked them to check for the lights, make sure all were still burning.

After a moment, the radio buzzed. "We've got the groundkeep down here. He says they don't use those lights you're talking about. Only these along the walkway."

Jeff could see the officer swing his arm, indicating the lanterns on posts that led toward the pool.

Brookner said, "Maybe she had on a sparkly ring, or she was holding a drink. You said it was late. Maybe she had a flashlight."

"I don't think so. You usually point a flashlight toward the ground. I thought it was a lantern of some sort, and the stirring of the limbs blocked it now and then. It kept winking."

Brookner looked down at the scene. "You've got better eyesight than I do if you saw something from way up here. You through with them down there?"

Jeff nodded.

Brookner took the radio. "That's it, Dwight. Send them back up."

"May I have your attention, please?" The static voice came over the loudspeaker. "Would Mr. Jeffrey Talbot please call the front desk? There is a phone call for Jeffrey Talbot."

Jeff made his way to the lower level of the bar and identified himself. The bartender punched some numbers, then handed him the phone.

It was Sheila. "Jeff, thank God. Didn't they tell you earlier that it was urgent?"

"No. Are you okay?"

"Greer's back from the theater."

"Damn it, Sheila, bodies are falling around here like horseflies and you called to tell me that?"

"You know better, Jeff Talbot."

Jeff sighed heavily. "Sorry. It's just that —"

"Never mind. I'd forgotten that Greer picked up some German during those summers with his grandparents."

"And?"

"And, I told him about the document you found. You're never going to believe what a 'Schreibtisch' is."

"*Who*, Sheila. *Who* a Schreibtisch is."

"No, *what*. Some people think it's a couch, but it's not. It's a desk."

"So?"

"One of those vertical desks with the drawers down one side. Jeff, a davenport."

Chapter Twenty-six

Cal Brookner let out a low whistle. "You don't say? So this Eric von Schreibtisch and Edward Davenport were the same person."

Brookner and Talbot were seated once again in the interrogation room. Jeff hadn't wanted to give the detective this latest news with everyone else around.

"Could be," Jeff said. "Could also be a coincidence."

"Yeah, it could be, but I've been in law enforcement for over twenty years, and I haven't seen a coincidence yet." Brookner pondered a moment. "We'll run it down, sure, but in the meantime, I'm gonna proceed under the assumption that Davenport and Schreibtisch are one and the same."

"If it's true," Jeff said, "it'll make things a hell of a lot easier. In any event, it looks like there was a connection between Hamilton and Davenport, probably related to something here — either the festival or some deal they'd made for an antique. It might have had nothing to do with the festival, specifically, but this was a good place to meet. No one would be suspicious, since it's the line of work they were both in."

The detective toyed with an unlit cigarette. "Hamilton must have found out about some secret life Davenport, or whoever the hell he was, was leading. Probably used the document you found as leverage. Sounds like blackmail to me, cut and dried."

Brookner stared down at a notepad on the desk as if it were a game card with Free in the center. He moved his right index finger around the notepad, touching first this square, then that. Jeff practically heard the caller's voice echoing out B-11, N-28, G-41.

Jeff had been there himself many times, concentrating, listening, waiting while a game of Blackout pulled your nerves tight as catgut. Every square had to be covered.

"Bingo!" Brookner slapped the table.

Jeff grinned.

Brookner didn't seem to notice. "Davenport resisted, Hamilton put on the pressure, and Davenport killed him. Later, he couldn't take the guilt, so he clocked himself." He stared expectantly at Jeff.

"Could be. But why? If that's true, don't you want to know why Hamilton was blackmailing him?"

"Not if no other crimes are committed. Since Davenport killed himself, I doubt that whatever scheme the two had cooked up ever took place."

"I'll admit you've got some valid arguments. But if Davenport killed himself, why isn't there a note? And what about the woman I saw? If what you say is true, then she could easily have something to do with it."

"Who knows? Could've been Hamilton's sister out for revenge. What's her name? Bliss? Bass — ?"

"Blessing. Trudy Blessing." Jeff thought about his conversation with Trudy. "No, I don't buy it. She doesn't have the stomach for it. Besides, I saw her when she heard her brother was dead. She was genuinely shook up."

"Talbot, listen. Before, I had two bodies and a string of ifs, ands, and buts held to-gether with threads of cotton candy. Now I've got two bodies and a motive and a docu-ment to cement the connection between them. Oh, and don't forget the murder weapon. Forensics is still working that angle. I'll be surprised if they find any tissue or blood samples left on it, but who knows? My point is, why else would a lug wrench be in that fountain? *With* the body, I might add. And don't tell me it's another friggin' coinci-dence. I've got a guy with a reputation for a temper and another guy who, if you think about it, probably didn't have the stomach for murder, either.

"But boil it down: Davenport felt trapped. He reacted, killed Hamilton. Most likely, it wasn't premeditated. Just one of those times when things got out of hand. He saw the lug wrench on the ground and . . . well, you know how the old story goes.

"Next day, Davenport tries to go about things in a normal manner. Breakfast with friends, his lecture. He really liked the spotlight, didn't he? Well, we put him in the spotlight that morning — hit him pretty hard when we interrogated him. With good reason, so it seems. He must've panicked. Didn't think a one-horse town — get it? One-horse town? — could play with the big boys." Brookner stopped, took a deep breath, then let it out in a rush. "Well. Game over."

Jeff's lips tightened. "Would you at least try to track down why Davenport — Schreibtisch, rather — left Germany? It's out of the Bureau's jurisdiction, and I don't have a fishing buddy with the CIA."

"Any other requests, Talbot?" Brookner's voice had an edge to it. "You're on a roll."

"Yes. I'd like to know where the lug wrench came from. Have you checked with the grounds crew? Yesterday I heard a kid getting chewed out for leaving hedge clippers lying on the ground. It may be as simple as someone losing his temper while changing a tire on one of those commercial mowers and throwing the lug wrench in the fountain."

"You've got a point. I'll put Littlefield on that."

"And another thing I want to know is who the mystery woman was. What if she was Hamilton's partner?"

"What if she was? Nothing came of it, apparently. At least, not in my book." Brookner stood. "Like I told you before, I need this one stamped Case Closed. Mackinac Island pulls more tourist dollars than anything else up here, casinos included. If we can wrap this up with a big red bow on top and give it to the media, then we might nip everyone's fear in the bud."

Brookner left before Jeff had a chance to respond.

He didn't feel like being sociable, so he headed up to the fourth floor and went to his room.

The investigative part of his brain was overheated. With effort, he turned it off and directed his thoughts to the approaching auction.

As a teenager he'd once become too anxious and spent a lot more on a book press than it was worth because shills had been planted in the crowd to drive up the bids. Jeff's grandfather, who had taken him to the auction, had allowed this to happen, later explaining to the boy that it was a lesson he would not soon forget.

Jeff hadn't forgotten. He knew that in the heat of bidding, an auctioneer enjoyed ultimate control. This wasn't a problem unless the auctioneer was unscrupulous for one reason or another.

It doesn't matter that it stinks and that every-one in the room knows it.

The gavel comes down.

Sold!

The next item comes up for bid.

And that's what everyone is thinking about — everyone, that is, except the guy who just got screwed over. And who's paying attention to him?

The thing is done. It's like a fight that's been fixed. If the ref and the handlers and the announcers are moving things along in a commanding, professional manner, and the fighter himself claims it was fair and square, then there's not a hell of a lot anyone can do.

What if Edward Davenport *had* been on the take? He could just as easily have dropped the gavel early, in order to ensure that a certain person was high bidder on a certain item, as he could've held out longer than he should've for more bidding. Jeff had witnessed both practices, and they weren't easy to contest due to an auction's quick pace and an auctioneer's even quicker chatter.

The phone rang. Jeff was getting sick of the thing. Hell, he didn't get this many calls in a week's time at home.

"Jeffrey?" It was Blanche.

"You've got your ESP in full swing," Jeff said. "I was about to call you."

"Jeffrey, have you talked to Trudy? I've been trying to reach her, but her hotel doesn't have phones in the rooms. Can you imagine that? A hotel room without a phone in this day and age."

"Maybe I should get a room over there. It'd be one way to get a night's sleep."

"Is that cynicism I hear in your voice?"

"Probably. I left a desk job so I wouldn't have to screw a phone to my ear forty hours a week."

"Is that all that's bothering you?"

"That, and a hundred other things." He told her about the document he'd found in Hamilton's room and the possibility that it would reveal Davenport's true identity. Then he told her about Brookner's reaction, including his announcement that the investigation was over. "It's too easy," Jeff concluded. "It may be true, but, if you want my opinion, there are still too many questions left unanswered."

"Sounds like it. Do you have any theories?"

"Still working on it. I did have an interesting visit with Trudy earlier. Did you know she was Hamilton's sister?"

No response.

"Blanche?"

"That's why I've been trying to reach her. I've been worried sick. I desperately wanted to ask you earlier whether anyone had told Trudy about Frank's death, but I couldn't break her confidence in me. You understand, don't you? I would do the same for you."

"I know. And you have several times." Jeff knew that Blanche had never spoken to anyone about Sheila.

Jeff explained to Blanche what had happened earlier with Trudy. He told her about learning that Jennifer Hurst had once been engaged to Frank Hamilton. He concluded with a question. "Why don't they have the same last name?"

"That I can tell you. They're actually half brother and sister. Same mother, not the same father. She always liked to think she had one pure and true connection to *somebody*. Frank was the only candidate."

"I'm beginning to wonder if anyone is who he says he is."

"No one ever is."

"That's a hard one to swallow. It would be like saying you could've done it."

"Don't underestimate me, Jeffrey. If my life were in danger, or if some kind of rage was driving me, I could do things that would make your blood run cold."

Jeff was quiet. He couldn't tell whether Blanche was being serious or merely trying to make a point. Damned telephone. "Remind me to try and stay on your good side," he said with a laugh.

Her dark mood didn't budge. "Remember, Jeffrey. Anyone can commit murder. Anyone."

He knew she was right, and he told her so. With nothing else left to cover, they said their good nights and he cradled the receiver.

He'd been going nonstop for damn near twenty hours. Worse, he was supposed to return home in twelve, although he wasn't sure how that would pan out if he got closer to solving the case. Or, cases. What were his chances of solving the mystery of the woman in the hat? Even if he worked as steadily as a clock's second hand — without any of the sleep his body was aching for — his chances were slim at best. He wished he could stay awake, wished he could operate on no sleep. It bothered him that he would spend half of his remaining time here dead to the world. But he was exhausted. And besides, he figured everyone else was already in dreamland. There wasn't much else to do on the quiet island. Since he couldn't tap into the dreams of those on his suspect list, he may as well join them, if only for a few hours.

The knock on the door didn't come as an urgent pounding, but it wasn't tentative, either. Sharp, to the point, decisive. Jeff bolted upright in bed, instantly awake. His sleep had contained no dreams — none he was aware of, anyway, in spite of the medical field's claims that everyone dreamt, always — so the rap at his door didn't come to him with the startling crack of a bolt of lightning. It didn't come as gunshots, either. It wasn't a car backfiring (do they even do that nowadays?) or a bowling ball making a strike, or even a bowling ball bouncing down a flight of stairs, for that matter. There was no swimming up from the deep, no disorientation where you stumble out of bed without a clue as to what city you're in. The only thing he could blame on waking him was that damn knocking at the door.

He got there in less time than it would have taken to say "just a minute" and looked through the peephole. A woman stood on the other side staring back at him.

So close was she to the fisheye that it distorted her features, giving her a nose like Cyrano, eyes set wide apart and slanted as if they wrapped around her head, and little ears the size of thimbles.

He opened the door.

"Mr. Talbot. I must talk to you."

Jeff, who was accustomed to noting details in order to deliver the outside world back to his housebound wife, keenly observed the person who stood before him.

With the convex distortion removed, the woman's straight nose was still slightly large, but with contouring she had created an illusion that it was in proper proportion to the rest of her face. It hadn't been altered by cosmetic surgery. Had there been repairs, he had no doubt he would have seen them in the same way he would detect signs of repairs on a chair leg or the leaf of a table.

The woman's complexion shone like porcelain; she obviously tended it with an eye to the future, a knowledge of the value of proper maintenance. She was probably looking at thirty-five, and the way she held herself suggested she would meet it head on. She was the type who had her bag of tricks ready and adjusted its contents when the elements or climate or stress or birthdays threatened to mar the finish that was her.

Her hair was done in rich, appealing shades of auburn, an expert blend of hennas not to be found simply in nature — or in the contents of a solitary bottle. Jeff suspected she was covering an onset of premature silver that might easily have been inherited.

She wore an unstructured box jacket in something soft and inviting — that sensuous chenille that Sheila had taken to wearing — in navy over a taupe ribbed jersey pullover. She was of slender build and when the jacket fell away from her body, he noticed that her form barely caused a spread of the ribbing at the bustline. Her navy Dockers were flat-fronted, continuing the long, slender line. All that blue only added to the startling effect of her eyes. They were like electric sapphires.

Jeff smiled, extended his hand. "We haven't met."

She took his hand, held it. "I'm Ingrid Schreibtisch. Edward Davenport's daughter."

Chapter Twenty-seven

Jeff blinked. Brookner's hunch had been right. The name was no coincidence.

"Actually," she said, "it's Ingrid Schreiber. I changed it when I went into business for myself," she explained as she settled into one of two wing chairs near the French doors that led to the balcony. Her German accent lent gravity to her speech.

"What business is that?" He had pulled a robe on over his pajamas after inviting her in and was putting coffee on to brew. Answers had come to his doorstep in a five-foot-nine package and he wanted to make sure he stayed alert.

"Ingrid's. It's a chain of beauty salons I began in Europe ten years ago. Three will be opening here in the States in time for the holidays."

Beauty salons. Jeff thought how appropriate this was, as if she'd inherited her father's antique sense and applied it to people. Objects and humans both required proper care in order to last.

"You are part of the antique world, aren't you, Mr. Talbot?"

"I'm a picker. As much for myself as for clients, if I'm not careful." He placed two steaming mugs on the small table beside her, then seated himself in the other chair. "Did your father tell you much about the business?"

"Yes." Her gaze rested on his bruise, but she made no comment. She sipped from the mug, testing the liquid's heat, then took a healthy drink.

She looked fresh and alert, even though it was three hours before sunrise. Jeff wondered if her inner clock was set by some time zone across the Atlantic, or if she was simply a morning person. His own inner clock was always set to Pacific Java Time.

"A picker." She said it as if she was scrolling through some mental dictionary for a definition. "You'll want the provenance then. The story of how this all started, of what led to . . . to his death." She looked up. "This is very difficult, Mr. Talbot. I've never told anyone what I'm about to tell you."

"Then why *are* you telling me?"

"I overheard you earlier, in the bar upstairs. You were talking to that detective."

"Brookner."

"I don't know his name. But I do know he's wrong."

"Wrong? What about?"

"About who killed Frank Hamilton."

Jeff fought the urge to bolt from his seat

shouting, *I knew it!* He leaned forward. "You're saying Edward Davenport *didn't* kill Hamilton."

"Yes."

"Do you have proof?"

She paused. "It's hard to say. Probably not anything that will withstand scrutiny, but I'm not sure about your American laws."

"Let's back up. Tell me what happened, and we'll go from there, okay?"

"As I said, there is a provenance. It's the only way you'll understand why things escalated to my father's taking his own life."

"I'm not convinced he took his own life."

"He took his own life. I'm sure of it. But not for the reasons that detective believes. My father's tragedy began more than twenty years ago."

She took several deep breaths. Jeff kept quiet. Someone was about to let a great deal of light into a room that had been dark for a lifetime.

"My parents' personalities were directly opposed. My mother was a strong-willed woman, and she ruled everyone around her: my father, the household staff, me.

"I was an only child. When I should have been with other girls my age — playing with dolls or sharing diaries or whatever it is young girls do — I was at home. My mother explained that my duty was to her, so I was always trying to please her, always afraid that

I would do something that would set her off. Like many children put under that kind of pressure, I believed I was the root of her anger, her disappointment. If only I could be a better daughter, I thought, things would improve.

"My parents had a disastrous marriage. I always wondered why Father didn't just leave. I believed he had a choice where I didn't.

"Something happened when I was twelve. Mother accused him of an unforgivable sin.

"Finally, he'd had enough. He told her he was leaving, and that he was taking me with him. That way she would have complete freedom to do whatever it was she thought she was missing.

"She went into a rage, told him he could leave but that she'd never give up her rights to me. At the time, it was as if she was saying for the first time that she loved me. She wanted me. Looking back, I realize she was merely using me in an effort to control my father.

"Things got worse until finally she told me that she had devised a way to drive him out of Germany."

A shuffling noise came from the doorway. Both of them jumped. Jeff went to the door. On the floor was the morning's *New York Times* and the hotel's daily schedule. That put the time around four a.m. He explained the practice to Ingrid. He wanted her to relax and feel comfortable continuing her story.

She asked for more coffee. He poured for them both, then took his seat. "She decided to force your father to leave Germany," he prompted.

"Yes. She accused my father of . . . things. Even after years of therapy, it is difficult to talk about. And I *can't* repeat all the shameful words she used when she confronted him. I believe the American word is *molest?*"

Jeff nodded solemnly.

"She accused him of molesting me."

"*She* accused. Not you."

"Not me." Ingrid's voice carried conviction. Then her gaze fell to the floor. "Not at first. Later, she forced me to say it. When I did, she told him if he would leave us alone — leave Germany altogether — that legal charges would not be brought up against him.

"I learned much later that she'd made him sign some sort of document, an admission of guilt. It also stated that, because of his confession, she would not bring legal charges as long as he never attempted to contact me."

She sat with her arms wrapped around herself, legs crossed, as if drawing in to herself.

Jeff remained quiet, gave her space. He thought she might cry, but she didn't.

At length, she went on. "I can't explain

why I lied for her. My therapist calls it . . . I don't know, something about the mother and child relationship and how I had always been taught to obey her. I felt I had no choice. Besides, she told me that it was only to make my father do as he was supposed to do, that it would have no long-term effects."

She laughed bitterly. "It's amazing, isn't it? What a domineering parent can convince you of? No long-term effects. Sounds like a medical phrase. I suppose it is, because my therapist has spent the last several years assuring me that he can help me get past the long-term effects.

"I lived under my mother's control until she died ten years ago. It was only after her death that I learned the particulars of her scheme. That's when I started searching for my father. I hired private detectives, checked universities on my own to try to learn where he had found a position. Of course, I thought he was still somewhere in Europe. It never entered my mind that he might have gone into another field, taken on a new identity, started a new life in another country. As you have guessed by now, I was quite the sheltered, naïve girl.

"Things changed finally with an odd stroke of fate." She repositioned herself in the chair, as if signaling a new direction. "I was at La Guardia about a year ago, waiting for a flight to Paris, when I saw his photo on the cover of *New York Monthly*. There was no doubt it was my father." She smiled. "It was like looking in a mirror. The article inside reported that he was as much a fixture of the city as Liberty herself. What a fitting thing to say, don't you think? He came here for liberty, for freedom. And he found it, too. For a while, anyway. Then he received a phone call from the man you found in the fountain.

"Father told me about it. Hamilton had gotten proof of his true identity. Years ago, a woman on my mother's serving staff stole the paper Father had signed. She then used it to blackmail my mother. My mother paid for years, in order to avoid scandal. Ironic, no? Her own weapon of blackmail was used against her. Eventually, the paper ended up in someone else's hands who sold it to Frank Hamilton.

"After we heard that Hamilton was dead, I tried to convince Father that the nightmare was over. I was sure no one else knew why he'd left the university and, finally, Europe.

"We spent much time together after I located him. In ways, we made up for the lost years." She shrugged. "Even though we weren't close, like a father and daughter should be, we had found a peaceful place. I wasn't prepared to lose him so quickly. He lived in fear of the accusations, even after I told him that my mother was dead.

"He told me that in time he had begun to

266

relax. He really believed he had created such a different life, a different identity, that he couldn't be traced to Ilke Screibtisch in a place and time as far removed as Germany.

"I tried to convince him that we didn't need to hide. He had done nothing wrong. But he couldn't get past the fact that he had allowed her to pressure him into signing that contemptible confession.

"He had so completely become this alter ego that he believed Eric Von Schreibtisch was buried forever. I thought so, too, when I could not locate him.

"He was a noble man, Mr. Talbot. He suffered greatly at the hands of my mother. I begged her on her deathbed to tell me where he was, to tell me why she had used me to ruin his life. She refused to answer, dying instead with a firm grip on her bitterness. That is when I tried to find him, using most of my inheritance. After paying the last of a long line of investigators, I used what was left to open my first shop. In an odd way, you see, my inheritance helped me find him after all.

"That brings us to Mackinac Island. I decided to surprise him by visiting him here. He's subject to mood swings, but I've never seen him as distraught as he was when I arrived. He finally admitted that he was being blackmailed by someone attending the festival."

Jeff realized he'd been leaning forward. He

sat back. "Are you aware he was on medication?"

"Yes. He had been fighting high blood pressure."

"Ingrid, the medical examiner found only one prescription in your father's things. It was for manic depression."

Ingrid was silent for a moment. "So, in addition to blackmail, first by my mother and then by someone here, he wasn't mentally stable."

"Probably not. He was drinking, too. With what you've told me, it sounds like he felt he had nowhere else to turn."

"Mr. Talbot, I was with my father the night Frank Hamilton was killed. I realize you have only my word to go on, but I assure you my father was not a murderer."

Jeff wanted to believe her. Just as he wanted to believe that none of the other suspects were murderers. "If you had absolved him in the accusations from when you were a young girl, why would he kill himself?"

"I've been trying to figure that out. He was very distraught Saturday after the police interrogated him. He got a call right after returning to the room, but I'm not sure who it was from. All he said was that Hamilton had told someone else about the documents. He panicked, speculated that any number of people might know about his past.

"I told him it didn't matter, that I could

tell them what my mother had done. He wouldn't hear of it. He said that the media would get hold of it, sensationalize it, ruin my life and my business. My shops here in the States would be doomed before they even opened. I tried to convince him that I didn't care, but he wouldn't listen."

"What about a note? Do you have one?"

"No. But I think there was one. He always traveled with his personal stationery. Saturday morning he remarked that he only had three sheets left. After the police left, I checked his things. There were only two sheets on the desk."

"How did you get into his room?"

"My father gave me a key. Yellow tape is easy to walk under, even when you're as tall as I am." She shrugged one shoulder. "At any rate, I don't think the police would have taken a sheet of the stationery or used it to make notes on. But I haven't contacted them. I didn't know what to do."

"Detective Brookner is convinced your father killed Hamilton. You're the only witness who can deny that."

"There's another witness who knows he didn't do it."

"Another witness?"

"Of course," she said. "The murderer."

Chapter Twenty-eight

"You realize you're going to have to talk to the police."

She nodded. "I also realize I'll be a suspect. I probably have as sound a reason as anyone to want Hamilton dead. That is why you must get the police to continue their investigation, Mr. Talbot. My father is innocent . . . innocent of everything he's been accused of. More innocent than his own daughter. I have done some horrible things — things that altered lives forever. But *take* a life? That is something I did not do. I need help convincing your detective of that."

Jeff studied the woman across from him. He couldn't say why, but he was convinced. "We have to get Brookner to keep looking for some evidence."

He called the island's police department and was surprised to learn that Brookner was there. When the detective came on the line, Jeff asked if he'd made it over to the mainland the night before.

"Nah. Too much paperwork here, so I crashed in the holding cell."

"Don't get too comfortable. Before you

270

stamp Case Closed on your box, I've got someone else for you to talk to."

"Talbot, don't you ever give up? By now the wires have picked up our story, and every Sunday paper worth reading is telling tourists that Mackinac Island is the safest place to visit this side of Disneyland."

Jeff paused for effect. He also wanted to make sure he had Brookner's attention. "I've got Edward Davenport's daughter in my room."

The silence that filled the phone wires was long enough to make Jeff wonder if the connection had been broken. Finally, Brookner said, "Is her last name Schreibtisch?"

"Yes, it is."

"You see, Talbot? No coincidences."

Jeff let him have that one.

Brookner asked, "Can you keep her there?"

"Not a problem. She wants to talk to you."

"What does she want to do, confess?"

"To the murder? No."

"Been practicing cryptic, Talbot?"

"Even if I told you, you'd have to hear it again from her. I have to catch a plane out of Pellston sometime today."

"Well, God knows I don't want you to miss it. Sometimes you make my ass twitch."

"French Kiss."

"What?"

"Sorry. I thought you were quoting a line from a movie."

Brookner dropped it. "Give me five minutes. I'll have Mel drive me up in the Explorer."

"Good. I'd hate for a day to go by without my seeing a motorized vehicle up here."

"Smart ass." The phone clicked and blew Jeff a raspberry, as if to remind him he was still on Brookner's turf.

Jeff told Ingrid that the detective was on his way. He then grabbed trousers and a blue oxford shirt from the closet and went into the bathroom to change.

He glanced in the mirror. His face looked like hell. He needed to shave, and the scratch on his cheek was now bright red, surrounded by a bruise that resembled a wine stain.

After escorting Ingrid to the interrogation room and introducing her to Brookner and Littlefield, Jeff made his way to the dining room.

The maître d' escorted him down the center aisle and seated him at a table for two near the bandstand. Jeff could only assume that they'd walked him back that far because they had more time to do so. In another fifteen minutes, the place would likely be buzzing with guests having breakfast and making arrangements to ferry back to the mainland.

Along with coffee, he ordered eggs Benedict and orange juice. He would need all the jolts they could offer: caffeine, protein, vitamin C. His nerves were on edge, knowing that he would have to leave the island in five hours — short hours if you were trying to squeeze in the last of a vacation; even shorter if you had a long list of murder suspects also preparing to leave. He didn't have a single thread to grab onto.

He was so lost in his thoughts, going over every bit of information he had, that he hadn't noticed others in the massive room.

When a waiter brought around more coffee, Jeff surfaced and looked around. Here and there were people he'd seen over the course of the Antiques Festival, ones that left about as much of an impression as milquetoast would have on the hotel's elaborate menu. His gaze rested on the back of an old man seated near the entrance. As his mind worked its way around to his initial reason for being here, Jeff tried to determine if it was Pettigrew, the old man who had shown him the cabaret set.

A moment of panic gripped him. He checked his watch. Although it was early, he felt as if he were in some sort of time warp. The cabaret set was to be auctioned at ten. He'd felt that he somehow had missed the one thing he desired most from this trip: to acquire the royal tea set that had left Blanche's possession nearly sixty years ago.

A member of the hotel staff approached

the old man and handed him a cordless phone. He listened, nodded twice. Then he slouched, combed the long white nails of a trembling hand through his white hair. It was him. It was Curtis Pettigrew.

The staff member gingerly took the phone, then placed a palm against the old man's back and said something. The old man nodded, rose from his chair and left the room.

Jeff wondered what that was about. It was obvious that he'd received some disturbing news. Was something up with the cabaret set? Did he need someone to be with him? Compelled to make sure the old man was all right, Jeff started toward the door.

He caught sight of Pettigrew going out of the building. He started to follow, but then held back, unsure of what he might say, of whether he would be intruding. He couldn't just go up to him and say, "You seemed disturbed after your phone call in the dining room," or, "Do you need help with anything?"

After debating the issue for a moment, he asked himself *Why not? Why can't I show concern?* Earlier, after the old man had invited him in to see the cabaret set, Jeff had been aggravated with himself for being off his game. He'd checked back later, but the room was locked up. He'd knocked, but no one answered. Why hadn't he thought to ask the basic questions a picker asks: How did you come about owning it? Why are you selling now? How long ago did you acquire it? Did you purchase it from a shop? An individual? Who? *I must be losing my edge,* he had thought.

Now, fate was giving him a second chance, and he was not about to let it get away.

He went out the Parlor doors and down the stairs. Pettigrew was nowhere in sight. He couldn't have moved that fast. Jeff darted back up the stairs and checked the porch. The old man wasn't there.

He started back down the stairs, more slowly this time.

"Do you need some assistance, sir?" A young man in red tails and top hat was standing behind a podium at ground level.

"An elderly gentleman just came out this way, but I've lost him."

"Yes, I helped him down the stairs." The young man nodded toward the almost-hidden staircase that led to the Tea Garden. "He started toward the Labyrinth."

Chapter Twenty-nine

Jeff hurried across the lane. At the bottom of the stairs, he consulted his booklet. There it was, a labyrinth to the west of the gardens. He hadn't noticed it before.

The dense, green lawn glistened, still wet from last night's rain. Jeff made his way toward a thick stand of trees to the west, following a dark trail where the water had been sluiced away from the grasses' blades. The pursuit reminded him of his grandfather. Mercer Talbot seemed ancient when Jeff was a boy. Crooked from arthritis and relying heavily on a wheeled, metal walker, he moved at a snail's pace when Jeff was required to walk alongside him. But if Jeff *wanted* to join in? It was like running a damn foot race to catch up with the old man.

Trying to reach Curtis Pettigrew was no different. The man was nowhere in sight. Jeff entered the Labyrinth and turned right into the disk-shaped maze.

He circled, listening to Lake Huron's waves slap the beach. The occasional seagull cry rose above the muted thunder of the waves, the only sounds present, filling the senses completely, as if nothing else existed for a thousand miles. He thought of the Pacific Coast. Home. He'd be damn glad to get back there. Never had a trip felt as drawn out as this one. When he got together with buddies for weekend fishing trips — long, quiet days on the dock or in the boat and loud nights of coffee and fish frying outdoors and, later, whiskey and poker — the hours slid away. The last forty-eight hours here had been an endless chain of stress-filled moments, all somehow linked to the cabaret set.

Ahead was a stone bench. Pettigrew was seated there, head stooped, still, unmoving. He looked as if he'd always been there, carved statuary from ages past, captured by the eerie song of the waves.

Jeff debated how to approach the old man. He didn't want to startle him, and he wasn't sure how to go about getting his attention.

He waited. The lyric lapping of waves against shoreline lulled him, mesmerized him, toyed with his body's lack of sleep. He drifted, swayed.

"What the hell do you want?" The old man shouted over the pounding of the waves against the shore.

Jeff jerked. "Mr. Pettigrew. You looked upset. I saw you at breakfast. But I can leave if you wish to be alone."

"Isn't that what a labyrinth is for?" He

pulled his heavy sweater closer about him and looked away.

"Yes, it is. And I'm sorry I intruded. I just wanted to make sure you were all right." Jeff turned to go.

"Josephine is dead."

Jeff turned back. Not only was the old man distraught, but he was also senile. He'd said the same thing when Jeff first met him in the Pavilion where the auction items were displayed. Jeff walked toward him. "Yes, sir. We talked about that yesterday, remember?"

"No, *my* Josephine. My wife, Josie." The old man bowed his head. "I got the call a few minutes ago."

Jeff thought of Sheila, of how it would feel to learn she had died when he was across the country. "I'm truly sorry, Mr. Pettigrew."

"Do I know you?" He peered at Jeff. Slowly, the veil of confusion lifted, then the gray eyes cleared as if recognition had sharpened their tint. "You're the young man with Josephine's letter. Jeff, isn't it?"

"Right on both counts."

"Then we should talk." The man scooted to one end of the bench.

Jeff noticed that the man wasn't wearing his ill-fitting dentures. Meals must have been easier to manage without them.

"Are you married, Jeff?"

Although Jeff made it a point never to talk about Sheila, he couldn't bring himself to lie to this old gentleman. "Yes. Very happily, as a matter of fact."

"Happily? Well, you're both young. You have your health."

Jeff wasn't sure why, but he was overcome with a need to tell this man about Sheila. Perhaps it was because he'd thought so much about her on this trip. Or maybe it was because he rarely talked to anyone about his situation at home. "Physically, yes. Mr. Pettigrew, my wife's an agoraphobic. She's —" he thought how best to say it so the old man would have a true picture — "she's a shut-in. She hasn't been out of our home in over five years."

"I see."

Jeff doubted it.

"Then you will understand what I'm about to tell you. My wife has been fighting cancer for a very long time. Surgeries, chemo, enough prescriptions to start our own pharmacy. It's been a struggle, living off our savings and the pitiful amount we get from Social Security." He turned to Jeff with an angry face. "Don't pay into it, my boy. You're better off stuffing greenbacks into your mattress."

His expression softened again. "Anyhow, funds were dwindling fast. The tea set was the only thing we had left to get any money out of. My wife loves that tea set. It's been hers since I bought it from a fella named Odom back in the forties. Anyhow, the no-

279

tion of selling it damn near killed her. And it was her that came up with the idea. But, as she got worse, she figured it wouldn't do her any good if she was dead.

"Never did use the thing. Oh, she would take the pieces out of the case every couple months. 'Have to let the silk breathe,' she would say. But she wouldn't take tea from it. So, finally, she told me to see what we could get for it. Lucky for me, I was acquainted with an honest man who works at the museum where we live. He looked in the case and started suckin' in air and jitterin' around till I thought I was gonna have to call nine-one-one." The old man chuckled and looked at Jeff. "Hell, I didn't know what the big deal was."

"You're kidding." Jeff couldn't imagine paying a hefty sum for something without having some idea of its provenance or, at the very least, its value. He assumed, anyway, that the set had cost plenty, even in the forties. "Weren't you told anything about it when you bought it?"

"Oh, sure. But I thought the guy was playing it up, you know? He tried to tell me how famous it was. His wife had just died, so I just figured he needed the money." Pettigrew was thoughtful for a moment. "Well, now, ain't that somethin'? I guess he needed the money then like I need it now. Or, like I needed it.

"I remember now, feelin' sorry for him. Those girls sure got a kick out of the tea set, and I hated to see him sell it. But it was his decision to make, and after his missus passed, he said he didn't like old things anyway. I thought he was just trying to cover up the fact that he needed money to raise his family. Josie and I had just got married, so I reckoned it would be a right nice present. And with the story and all fittin' her name. Well, you can see why I went ahead and bought it.

"The night before I left to come up here, I served her tea in it. She was so weak, she was afraid to try and hold the cup. So I held it for her. She was only able to take a couple sips, but you should of seen her face. Her cheeks got pink and her eyes twinkled . . . looked like she did the night I brought it home."

Both men sat quietly, each lost in his own thoughts. Jeff sensed that Pettigrew was in a place and time half a century ago. He was in his own place, a more recent place than Pettigrew's, when he and Sheila walked on the beach and watched the fishing boats glide in from the outer reaches of Puget Sound.

"Well." The old man's voice broke the spell, carrying with it a tone of finality. "I didn't want to leave Josie to come here, but she insisted. Said we'd already agreed to put the tea set in the auction. I didn't realize it till just now, but I suppose we said our good-byes before I left."

"Maybe that's the way she wanted it."

Pettigrew nodded, but he didn't appear to have heard what Jeff said.

"I've been thinking about that story you told me, and about that letter." His expression brightened into something Jeff recognized. Our strongest emotion as humans, Jeff believed, if for no other reason than its eternal link to the future. It was hope, and the old man's face was filled with it. "You *really* think that letter was written by the empress herself?"

Jeff smiled genuinely. "Yes, sir. Without a doubt. It's been analyzed by experts, both here and in Europe."

Pettigrew shook his head. "Hard for me to grasp. 'Course I've spent years telling myself that Odom's story was made up."

Jeff didn't look forward to the job he would have of filling in the blanks of the tea set's provenance. He wondered absently how many names had followed Blanche Appleby's family. To Pettigrew, he said, "Apparently, the man didn't know about the letter — or, more likely, how important it is.

"Once," Jeff continued, "I paid over two thousand dollars for a *piece* of a bit that had been used on one of Napoleon's horses. Napoleon probably had never touched the thing. He would've had a livery staff seeing to the livestock. Yet, he'd ridden the horse, and the papers proved it. The client I was representing thought he'd made a steal."

"When I hooked up with Davenport," Pettigrew said, "he told me there would be a lot of interest in the set, said I'd make more money than I'd ever dreamed of." Pettigrew clasped his hands. "Well, I hear a replacement auctioneer made it in last night, so it'll all be over soon enough. By rights, though, you're the one should have it."

"Don't worry, Mr. Pettigrew. I'll be high bidder." As Jeff spoke, a piece of something Pettigrew had said earlier shifted in his thoughts. He nudged it across the puzzle-board surface of his mind, pushing it this way and that, trying it first in one hole and then another until it dropped into place. It bottomed out in the pit of his stomach.

If he wasn't mistaken, Frank Hamilton did have a partner. And that partner had killed him.

Chapter Thirty

Sometimes, by the sheer grace of God, a murder was solved without a grain of concrete evidence falling into the hands of the authorities. It might be in the form of a confession. Even that had its own set of headaches. The crazies, who confessed simply for the thrill of confessing or for some warped attempt at attention and notoriety, had to be weeded out from the innocents who confessed, with the motive of protecting a loved one.

Without those, you tried to solve it with the push. Turn up the heat. Trick the guilty. Let him think he was getting away with it, then with one well-placed kick, knock the props out from under him. Sneaky? Sure. But it could be done.

Jeff was running out of time. He needed to push the killer, get him to prove it. To do that, he needed a plan that would turn up the heat that had fed the fire that had fueled the killer. He needed to put the water back on to boil. He needed to make the kettle whistle till it screamed.

Working on a hunch, Jeff asked Curtis

Pettigrew a few more questions. Then he told the old man his suspicions. They worked out a strategy. After agreeing to meet in the Brighton Pavilion at nine o'clock, Jeff left Pettigrew in the Labyrinth and hurried back to the hotel.

He had a tea party to plan.

Chapter Thirty-one

"Talbot!"

Jeff wheeled.

Cal Brookner started toward him from the east end of the porch. He shifted a manila folder to his left hand, then plucked the cigarette from beneath his mustache with his right. "I've been looking everywhere for you. Where the hell have you been?"

The detective started to flick the half-smoked weed over the edge, then apparently thought better of it and sought out a stone urn. He vaulted the stick into the white sand.

Jeff wasn't comfortable talking in the openness of the porch. You never knew who might be on a balcony above you or at one of the windows that opened directly onto the porch from parlor level. He waited until the detective was next to him. "You've finished with Ingrid Schreiber. What do you think?"

"I think it looks like we've got a whole new case on our hands, and not just because of what she said." Brookner shuffled through papers in the folder, listing slightly to keep from spilling the flimsy manila's contents. He pulled a sheet out like he was performing a tablecloth magic act and presented it to Jeff.

"It's a fax," he went on. "Just came in from the lab up in Marquette."

Jeff studied it. "Says here there was no way the murder weapon was a lug wrench."

"Yeah. I should of known better, trying to wrap this up on account of political pressure. State tourism is one of the governor's pet projects."

Jeff continued reading. The report was typed professionally and used the typical terminology: Blunt-instrument blow to base of skull, severe but not isolated as probable cause of death. Massive contusion, right temple. Brain hemorrhage.

At the bottom, someone had scrawled *Cal, look in your crystal ball.*

"Crystal ball?"

Brookner shrugged. "Damned if I know what it means. I tried to call Nic, but she's out on another case. Assistant said she'd found something, though. It's being delivered from Marquette now. I sent Mel over to the mainland to intercept it."

Jeff pondered that a moment. "You asked where I'd been."

"Yeah. Is it worth repeating?"

Jeff told the detective about his conversation with Curtis Pettigrew. Some of it, anyway. He leaned in. "I'd like to follow a hunch. Are you willing to help me?"

"I'm willing to listen. Anything beats the

hell out of what I've got. There are too many connections to Hamilton, and in about three hours every damned one of 'em is going to scatter across that lake like ducks on opening day."

The two men went to the interrogation room and Jeff laid out his plan.

After he and Brookner met with hotel personnel, Jeff went to his room, made a phone call, then packed for the return trip home. He wouldn't have another chance after his plan was set into motion. If things went according to his calculations, he would draw out the murderer, attend the auction, and have just enough time to catch his ferry and make it to the Pellston airport.

He wanted to sleep. His body begged for it. But he knew if he gave in now, he'd be drained of the only thing that was keeping him on his feet. He couldn't afford to stop. He poured coffee on top of his adrenaline and went downstairs.

Chapter Thirty-two

The Brighton Pavilion, one of the larger rooms in the Woodfill Conference Center, gave one the feeling of being outdoors. The walls were light green — bright and fresh — with gleaming white trim. Suspended in a long row overhead were Venetian chandeliers in faceted glass of crystal and emerald, the glass pendants sparkling like dew-covered leaves in sunshine. Jeff had been in here once before, but he hadn't been aware of its color or design. He'd been too absorbed with the prospect of seeing the cabaret set for the very first time.

Even now, he saw the room as simply a flamboyant backdrop to a looming, dark scene.

Jeff walked in forty-five minutes before his guests were told to arrive. Several security guards were posted around the room.

Curtis Pettigrew had put in his dentures. The smile they created wasn't echoed in the old man's eyes. He was seated near the long display case in order to keep an eye on the cabaret set. Jeff's mind superimposed a vision over the scene, and he saw how Pettigrew would look in a few days, seated beside a casket that held the other treasure of his life. Jeff's heart went out to the old man. This must be a tremendous strain, having to wait before returning home to make arrangements for his wife's funeral. He walked over and stooped beside Pettigrew. "I want you to know, I appreciate your help with this. I couldn't pull it off without you."

"The Good Book tells us to let the dead bury the dead. I used to wonder what that meant, but now I know. I can't do anything to help Josie, but maybe I can do some good here." He leaned closer and Jeff saw a brief spark in the cloudy eyes. The old man whispered, "Besides, she'd love it that her tea set helped capture a criminal."

"Let's hope we make her proud, then."

Jeff discreetly checked behind a folding screen that concealed a service entrance to the room. He made sure the door was unlocked and was surprised to find that everything was already in order on the other side. After that, he arranged three small rows of chairs so that they faced the display case and podium.

The Pavilion's double doors opened, and Jeff watched as his guests began arriving.

Ben and Jennifer Hurst walked up and began admiring the set. The couple might not always get into the hunt, but it was rewarding to know they had an eye and a spirit for antiques.

Pettigrew was standing beside them, pointing out details. The couple oohed and ahhed over the set's unparalleled beauty, and Pettigrew's face was filled with something Jeff could only describe as a poignant mix of pride and pain.

They looked up and greeted Jeff as he approached.

"We were so excited to learn that the auction was being moved up," Jennifer said.

Jeff smiled. "I think several people feel the same way. I'm glad you made it."

"I wouldn't miss it." Jennifer turned back toward the display case. "I've never seen anything like it, have you? And to think that the Empress Josephine actually sat in her chambers in Paris and sipped tea from it."

"It's remarkable, isn't it? To know without doubt that these pieces were once in the presence of such astounding history."

"Excuse me."

Jeff turned toward the soft, tiny voice.

"Trudy! I was afraid you wouldn't get my message."

She smiled. "I got it a few minutes ago, Mr. Talbot. But what did you mean, 'We're having a tea party?' I'm sure you know it's not proper for morning."

Jeff laughed, then said to the others, "Shall we show her?"

All four of them pivoted away from the glass and stood two by two, creating a sort of wall on either side of the display.

Trudy's breath caught as if she'd just seen Moses part the waters.

Ben led her to the case, then said to Jeff, "I think we'll check out some of the other items."

Jennifer added a warning. "Don't start the bidding without us."

Trudy's eyes were wide with wonder. "Is it? Is it really Blanche's long-lost tea set?"

"Yes, it really is."

Wonder was replaced with urgency. "We have to get it back for her, Mr. Talbot. We just have to. Somehow."

"I'm going to try, Trudy."

"Trying isn't good enough."

"Trust me, Trudy, all right?"

"Okay, I'll try."

"Trying isn't good enough."

She only smiled, then took a seat in the back row.

Jeff looked several times for Asia Graham, Lily Chastain, and Ruth Ann Longan. The threesome wasn't there yet.

He watched Ingrid Schreiber walk in, carrying herself with a surety that didn't completely register in her vivid blue eyes. She was dressed in a similar ensemble to the one she wore when she'd come to his room earlier, only this one was black instead of navy. She, too, sat in the back row.

The Hursts took seats in the center row.

It was almost time to begin. Jeff was beginning to worry about the three older women when at last he saw tiny Ruth Ann walk through the door and then turn to look back like a mother duck checking on her brood. Eventually, Asia and Lily hobbled in on the black walking sticks they'd been carrying the night Jeff met them.

The three made their way slowly toward him. When they arrived, Asia and Lily dropped into two chairs in the front row, leaving a vacant one between them for Ruth Ann.

"I'm terribly sorry we kept you waiting, Jeffrey," Ruth Ann said. "It takes longer and longer for us to get everything packed and squared away."

"No need to apologize. I was only concerned that you'd run into problems."

Asia scooted around in the chair, obviously trying to find a comfortable position, and said, "No problems that a new odometer on an old body wouldn't fix."

Ruth Ann peered into the display case. "My, what a pretty thing." She turned to Jeff. "I don't understand why we were asked to be here, though. We don't really buy much porcelain."

Lily said, "Ruth Ann, speak for yourself. I told the gentleman who owns it that I might want a crack at it. You never know. It might go for a real bargain."

"But Lily," Ruth Ann said, looking closer at the tea set, "I don't see a single lily of the valley on it."

"Are you sure?" She leaned forward. "Isn't the young lady in the little boat holding a bouquet?" She didn't wait for a response before adding, "Well, we rushed around to get here early. We might as well stay."

"I suppose you're right." Asia checked her watch, then looked at Jeff. "What do you say we get on with it and boil this lobster?"

"You're right, Asia. Let's turn up the heat."

Chapter Thirty-three

"After visiting with Mr. Pettigrew this morning," Jeff began, "I learned that several of you are interested in purchasing the cabaret set. We could think of only one way to accomplish what needed to be accomplished where this set is concerned. That is why all of you were urged to attend this early auction.

"As some of you know, the set has a fascinating history — a history which, already full of dark turns, has taken on something new over the last few days. Its history now includes murder." Jeff glanced quickly from face to face. No one's expression gave away anything that might tell him what he was looking for. He continued.

"I've been working closely with Michigan authorities to establish a common link between the two men who died here this weekend."

"Why are you bringing up that horrible subject?" asked Jennifer. "Can't we just put that behind us and get on with the bidding?"

"I agree," said Lily. "Asia already told you we don't have much time. And I'm sure everyone here is in the same boat, so to speak." She swiveled and smiled at everyone, obviously pleased with her play on words.

Murmurs of agreement rose from the group.

"I'm in the same boat, as you so cleverly put it. If you'll just bear with me, this should only take a few minutes."

"Well," said Asia, "that depends on how tightly the pursestrings are drawn, don't you think?"

This brought a smattering of laughter, which Jeff suspected was as much a result of nerves as it was humor.

"Point taken, Asia."

Trudy half raised a hand. "But, Mr. Tal—"

"Trudy." It had come out more sharply than he intended. More softly, he said, "Bear with me, all right?" He had no doubt the girl was about to inquire how on earth he thought he could run the auction and bid for the tea set at the same time. She had a lot to learn about trust.

"The common link," he continued, "happens to be this very tea set."

More murmurs came from the group.

"It began when Frank Hamilton decided to blackmail Edward Davenport."

As the group reacted with varying degrees of surprise and dismay, Jeff studied each closely. Both Trudy and Ingrid bowed their heads slightly. Jeff figured Trudy's reaction was due to shame over her brother's ruthless-ness, while Ingrid's was from sadness over the loss of a father she'd only recently come to know. The rest of the group remained stone faced.

"Hamilton had uncovered a document proving that —" He paused, not wanting to reveal everything about Davenport — "proving something that gave him leverage over the auctioneer."

Jeff indicated the old man seated near the case. "While I was visiting with the set's owner, Curtis Pettigrew, he said something that reminded me of a fact I'd almost for-gotten. It has to do with the provenance of this set."

The door at the end of the room opened with a click. Everyone turned to see a female in a dark blue police uniform enter the room and walk quickly toward them.

Lily turned back to Jeff. "I really don't see why we need to hear all this gibberish."

Jeff didn't respond. Lieutenant Littlefield handed him a small envelope, then stood be-side him and waited. He opened it, pulled out a slip of paper with a small plastic evi-dence bag attached. Inside the bag, taped to a strip of pink litmus paper, was a tiny, clear sliver. Plastic, or maybe glass.

He remembered the note he'd seen earlier, the one written by the medical examiner. *Crystal ball.*

"Get on with the auction, why don't you?" Lily's voice held an edge.

Asia checked her watch again. "Calm down, Lily. We've still got time."

"There isn't going to be an auction." Jeff waited.

Ben and Jennifer Hurst turned confused looks on each other. Then everyone started talking at once, protesting.

Jeff shouted above them. "There isn't going to be an auction, because the set has already been sold."

"What? That can't be true. There has to be an auction." Lily grabbed her cane, her left hand wrapped around the collar and her right hand gripping the head just above the eagle's talons. As she hoisted herself from the chair, she let out a tiny yelp and let go with her right hand. She spread the hand, palm up, and investigated. She looked at Jeff.

He moved closer. There wasn't much blood on her hand, just a spot. "May I see your cane, Lily?" Jeff extended a hand.

She withdrew. "I'm perfectly capable of taking care of myself, young man."

"You've been taking care of yourself all your life, haven't you, Lily? Or, should I call you Margaret now? Now that I know you *are* Margaret."

"What? I don't know what you're talking about. My name is Lily Chastain."

"You felt like you had no choice. Am I right?"

"Mr. Talbot?" Ruth Ann said. "Have you taken leave of your senses? Her name is Lily Chastain. Why, Asia and I have known her since before you were born."

Jeff ignored her. "You knew Frank Hamilton, didn't you?"

"Why are you asking me these things?"

"You hired Hamilton, thinking that if he did the bidding for you, it would prevent any suspicion being directed toward you."

"Suspicion?" She laughed nervously. "Many people retain anonymity when purchasing rare antiques. If anyone should know that, you should." She stared at the clear baggie he was holding.

"Yes, I do. I also know that Hiram Odom —"

"Don't you dare mention that name to me." She raised her cane as if she were going to strike Jeff. "You don't know anything." The woman spat the words at him. She pulled the cane to her, gripped it tightly in both hands. "He was an evil, vindictive man. He ruined my life. He took the only thing that mattered to me, and do you know why? For *her*."

"Lily!" Asia shouted. "Honey, it's not worth it."

"Shut up, Asia. You're always goin' on about what was done to *your* people. You

299

never stop to think about how good you've had it. You haven't had to lift a finger your entire life. You got everything handed to you." She turned back to Jeff. "Did it matter to him that I was the one who loved him? That I was the one who took care of him after my mother died? I was the one who was supposed to get married. Not Blanche. But because she was the oldest, my father made me step aside. Well, my sister may have gotten George Appleby, but she's not going to get the tea set, too!"

She brought the cane over her head in an arc and struck the top of the display case. The tempered glass fractured into a mosaic of pebble-size discs. The case rattled and shuddered, and the discs hung together precariously above the porcelain.

Jeff moved in to stop her. Lieutenant Littlefield was already moving. Detective Brookner came from behind the Oriental screen.

Lily swung the cane again. Littlefield grabbed for it, but before she could get her hand around it, its collar popped off. The crystal sphere, still gripped by the ornamental claw, flew backward. The group of seated spectators scrambled for cover. A glass vial tumbled from the cane's handle, shattered against one of the chairs, and sent glass in every direction. A rolled piece of paper fell to the floor.

Brookner and Littlefield restrained Lily while Jeff picked up the scroll and shook shards of glass from its layers. He unfurled it, read it quickly, and handed it to Ingrid. "Is this your father's handwriting?"

Ingrid looked at the paper, then nodded. Trembling, she read what her father had written the day before. It took her a few moments to find her voice. Finally, she said, "I really didn't care what others thought. He should have believed me."

"Some parents do things in the name of love, others under the pressure of propriety. Do they use good judgment?" Jeff glanced at Lily. "Not always."

After several moments, Brookner walked over with the pieces from the cane.

"Take a look at this." He pointed to a spot where a small sliver of glass was missing. "I have no doubt that the glass taken from Hamilton's skull will fit right here."

Jeff took the handle and rotated the ball inside the talons. "It must've turned when she stood. That's how she cut her palm on it." When he started to give the ball back to Brookner, it picked up the light and winked.

"Well, I'll be damned," Brookner said. "I reckon that's what you saw Friday night."

"Probably so."

"You were right, Talbot. She just told me that she'd prearranged for Hamilton to get the tea set for her. Apparently, he had something on Davenport, told Chastain or Odom, or whoever the hell she is, that he would use it as leverage to rig the auction. Anyway, she's the one you saw in the garden. During her meeting with Hamilton, she let it slip that she was going to destroy the tea set. He reneged and they got into an argument. He stormed off, and she followed him."

"This was inside the cane." Ingrid showed the paper to Brookner.

"So there *was* a suicide note." Brookner read it, then grunted. "No wonder the old gal took it. This outlines her plan, Hamilton's involvement, and the part your father was to play."

"Apparently," Jeff said, "Lily Chastain didn't count on Hamilton's appreciation for antiques. I'd seen him before with treasures; he displayed a certain reverence for them. Too bad he wasn't the same way with people."

"Did she say how she got in the room?" Ingrid asked.

"The maid who found Davenport had left the door open when she ran for help. Mrs. Chastain saw her, and then it was a matter of right place, right time. She went in and saw the note, knew it would link her to Hamilton. So she grabbed it and got out of there before anyone arrived."

"Where did the lug wrench come in?"

"Closest thing to a coincidence we're

gonna get, Talbot," said the detective. "She found it on the ground, courtesy of your careless yard hand, and tossed it into the water to throw off the investigation. Of course, latent prints would've been nonexistent because of the water."

"They probably would've been anyway, detective. Lily Chastain is a proper Southern woman. She was wearing gloves that night."

Everyone looked toward the now silent Lily, who was slumped in a chair between Ruth Ann and Asia. Both women were talking to her in reassuring tones.

Trudy began crying softly. Jennifer put her arm around the girl's shoulders and held her.

Jeff returned to the podium. "May I have your attention, please? In order to uncover the truth, I asked the authorities to stage this early auction. The cabaret set has not been sold. It will be included in the auction beginning at ten o'clock, as originally planned."

Jeff went over to where Mr. Pettigrew was carefully removing the cabaret set from the damaged display case. Miraculously, the fragmented glass had not given way. It could, though, at any time. Piece by piece, the old man packed the set into the fitted Moroccan case that Napoleon had instructed be made from the finest leather and the best silk and the purest gold for the woman he loved.

"Josephine had it pretty good, didn't she?" Curtis Pettigrew said when he had finished.

"Yes, she did." Jeff added, "And I'm sure she told you that before you left on Friday."

The old man started to protest, then the sentiment sank in. He looked at Jeff and smiled.

Chapter Thirty-four

The plane taxied across the tarmac for what seemed like miles, then stopped as the pilot announced that they were eighth in line for takeoff.

Trudy broke a stick of gum out of its foil and popped it into her mouth. She gripped Jeff's arm tightly. Instinctively, his muscle tightened. She gasped. "I'm sorry, I thought I had the armrest. Are you okay?"

He chuckled, then assured her he was fine.

She began rubbing her arms, although she wore a heavy pink sweater over a matching turtleneck and a blue corduroy jumper.

"I can get a blanket for you, if you're cold."

"That's okay. I'm just nervous."

He had arranged to change seats to sit beside Trudy on the flight from Chicago to Seattle so that he could help her in case she needed anything. Also, he figured Trudy would eventually want to talk about what had happened. He wanted to be available when she did.

He was painfully aware of the vacant seat by the window to her right, where her brother should have been. Jeff felt a strange emptiness and realized that in the days and months to come, he would notice the absence of the young man at estate sales and antique shows.

The engines vibrated as the jet roared down the runway, picking up speed. The bird felt heavy when it lifted and put him in mind of a hawk that held too much dead weight in its talons but knew that if it let go, it might perish. The image of talons made him think of the murder weapon, and he wondered absently what would happen to it.

They climbed for several minutes before the plane leveled off and the roar changed octaves, moving to a higher pitch and quieting to something one might manage to talk over.

"How did you figure out it was Lily Chastain?"

He'd been right about her need for answers. He'd been watching her when she asked the question. She chewed vigorously on the gum, an odd counterpoint to the question concerning her brother's killer.

"When the man who owned the set, Mr. Pettigrew, started talking about old man Odom and his girls, I thought he meant Blanche and her mother. Then I started remembering some of the things Blanche told me the first time she told her story. She had a little sister. After that first time, Blanche never again mentioned her sister or her father or the fact that she'd never heard from her sister after that.

"When I called everyone this morning about the tea party, I put in a call to Blanche, too. That's when she told me her sister's name. Brookner was able to roust a clerk in Louisiana who blew the dust off a sixty-year-old record book and found where Margaret Odom had changed her name to Lily Oliver. She married Wiley Chastain a couple of months after that, adding just enough twists in the trail to slow down anyone who might be looking for her. The sad thing is, nobody was looking.

"Staging an auction was the only way I could think of to flush her out. It was a gamble."

"What will happen to her?" Trudy asked.

"Most likely, she didn't intend to kill your brother. Still, she's responsible for her actions. They'll charge her with involuntary manslaughter. I suppose the rest will depend on the judge and jury. Asia and Ruth Ann both said they'd do what they could to help her."

A shiver went over Trudy. "Sometimes, we see people like that at the shop. They become so obsessed with owning a certain item they nearly go insane."

"Helps you keep your priorities straight, doesn't it?"

Trudy agreed, then fell silent. After a while, she leaned her head against Jeff's shoulder and drifted off to sleep like a child.

She had more inner strength than she knew, Jeff decided, and she had Blanche on her side. She'd be fine.

When they stepped into the terminal at Sea-Tac, Jeff spied Greer waiting in his usual spot at the end of the walkway. He turned to Trudy. "Can we give you a lift?"

"I wouldn't want to be a bother."

"No bother at all."

Greer took Jeff's case. "Baggage claim, sir?"

Jeff laughed. "Have you ever known me to return without extra luggage?"

"No, sir."

As Trudy climbed into the woodie, she said, "Mr. Talbot, about your offer for Frank's funeral —"

"Trudy, that's been settled. I want to help."

Trudy rode without speaking, except to provide directions to her apartment. When Greer pulled the car up to the curb in front of the building, Jeff remembered what Jennifer had said about the renovated quarters where she'd met Trudy. From the looks of this building, Trudy's life hadn't changed significantly since then. Jeff told Greer to stay with the car, and he carried Trudy's luggage upstairs.

They stepped inside, and Trudy flipped the light switch. Jeff stopped in midstride. There were birdcages everywhere he looked: little ones grouped on tables and lined along shelves; large ones hanging from the ceiling; wooden ones, brass ones, wicker, of every architectural style imaginable. He recognized the Taj Mahal, Saint Basil's Cathedral, and Buckingham Palace. There were mansions too: Italianate villas, Georgian colonials, Gothic rectories, and every one built by hand. The place resembled a fabulous aviary, except for the complete absence of birds.

"Frank started this collection for me," Trudy said. "I wonder if he was aware of the symbolism to our relationship."

"Hard to say. He was a man of contradictions."

There was a brief silence. Then, without a word, Trudy moved from cage to cage and opened the delicate doors.

When Jeff went back downstairs, Greer was waiting beside the car.

"Greer, would it offend your butler's principles if I drove?"

"As you wish, sir."

At the end of two blocks, Jeff said, "Are you uncomfortable riding? You keep looking at me."

Greer hesitated, then said, "If I may ask, sir, what happened to your cheek?"

Jeff touched the scab. The brief altercation in the Rosalyn Carter Suite seemed decades ago. "You should see the other guy."

"Yes, sir."

"Greer, do you think you could drop the 'sir' for tonight? It's beginning to make me feel damned old."

"I'll try, sir."

Jeff heard music coming from upstairs. He found Sheila curled up in bed, watching a movie. On-screen, Christopher Reeve, in the costume of an Edwardian gentleman, was kissing Jane Seymour. It was *Somewhere in Time*. Sheila was crying.

Jeff joined her on the bed and handed her a tissue from the nightstand. "Honey, you've seen this movie a dozen times. I've never seen you cry over it before."

"I'm not crying over the damned movie."

He felt tired. He'd hoped they'd left the tension behind. "Are you still upset about before?"

"Not with you. I'm so glad you're home."

He put his arm around her. She leaned against him. "I just want to get better, Jeff."

"I know."

Chapter Thirty-five

Jeff parked the woodie, retrieved the case from the back, and walked the half block to the front entrance of All Things Old.

It seemed like ten years had passed since he'd left here Thursday evening.

Trudy was waiting for him as planned. She ushered him into her office next to Blanche's and stood watch at the door as he unpacked the pieces.

Constantly he reminded himself to remain steady as, one by one, he took each item from its protective wrapping and placed it on the large worktable. Then he assembled the pieces for presentation.

"Here she comes!" Trudy whispered excitedly.

Jeff followed suit, whispering, "Tell me when she's inside."

Trudy nodded.

After a moment, she turned. "Okay, she's in her office. Are you ready?"

Jeff exhaled, steadied himself. "I'm ready."

Trudy held the door open for Jeff as he maneuvered his way through the opening and into the corridor. He held back, then, while Trudy knocked.

"Come in." Blanche's voice sounded muffled, distracted, and Jeff knew that she'd already buried her head in the shop's ledgers. He followed Trudy inside.

Blanche was seated behind her desk, slippered feet planted as always upon her tapestry footstool. Her fiery red hair was piled high in curls that bobbed as she turned her head from receipts to columns and back again.

Something ached inside Jeff. How could he have ever suspected this virtuous woman of spying on him?

"Mrs. Appleby," Trudy said, "you may want to get out your checkbook. Mr. Talbot was high bidder on an auction item you'll be interested in."

Blanche looked up. Her jaw dropped, then clamped back shut. She clasped a delicate hand to her mouth. Tears welled in her eyes. At last, when she was able to speak, the words came out quietly and a little pinched by emotion.

"Oh my, oh my," she said.

Trudy, who'd been grinning broadly, suddenly burst into tears. With one hand she held the large frames of her glasses away from her cheeks and with the other dabbed at her eyes with a linen handkerchief.

Jeff placed the cabaret set on Blanche's desk. He swallowed hard, and a long moment passed before he could speak. "Have tea with us, won't you, Blanche?"

Blanche Appleby looked up at him with all the innocence and wonder of a child and nodded.

Recommendations from Jeffrey Talbot

Dear Reader,

As I replace reference books on the shelves of my library, I am compelled to share with you some comments on a few volumes you might enjoy. For those of you interested in learning more about antiques — or, more specifically, about some of the areas of collecting mentioned in my quest to attain Blanche's cabaret set — I encourage you to check out the following list. It's a bibliography of sorts, and includes my comments to help narrow your focus, if need be.

Sheila tells me there is such a thing as a "webliography" as well, and has asked that I list a few of her favorite web sites. (The things we do for love.)

Although Blanche's tea room, The Cabbage Rose, offers a near-infinite variety of coffees (thank God), it boasts many flavors of tea as well. As you've guessed by now, Blanche personally bucks our city's coffee tradition by consistently choosing leaves over beans. Since my trip centered around a tea set, I've agreed to include a couple of Blanche's favorite books on the ceremony of tea. (The things we do for friendship.)

By the way, I've shared my coffee bean combo with Blanche. She has named it "Jeffrey's Blend" and has added it to the tea room's menu.

Gordy Easthope and I are planning a fishing trip. Maybe I'll have a fish story or two to share with you next time out.

Meanwhile, best of luck keeping track of the bodies.

Jeff Talbot

The book in which Blanche found the pram is *Fine Wicker Furniture, 1870–1930*, by Tim Scott (Schiffer Publishing, 1990). It includes history, many color photographs, and a price guide. Remember to check publication dates and allow for changing market trends when considering the value of a piece you find listed in any book.

Antiques Roadshow Primer, edited by Carol Prisant (Workman Publishing, 1999). This volume from the hit PBS television show lives up to its name and is a great introductory guide. The show has become so popular, in fact, that its concept has been the subject of episodes of such popular sitcoms as *Frasier* and *Will & Grace*. (Since Sheila is housebound, we watch a lot of television and movies.)

The two books I found in Frank Hamilton's room are *The Bulfinch Illustrated Encyclopedia of Antiques*, Paul Atterbury and Lars Tharp, consulting editors (Bulfinch Press, First North American Paperback Edition, 1998), and *Warman's English & Continental Pottery & Porcelain* (3rd Edition), by Susan and Al Bagdade (Krause Publications, 1998). I find the Bulfinch volume to be a constant source of valuable information about everything from porcelain to furniture. Wonderfully categorized, it offers history, time line charts, and a wealth of color photographs. *Warman's* is a price guide with valuable information, including maker's marks and histories.

If my pursuit of the cabaret set whetted your appetite for more about Napoleon and Josephine, I recommend the definitive biography, *Napoleon Bonaparte*, by Alan Schom (HarperCollins, 1997).

Although *Inkwells II*, by Veldon Badders (Collector Books, 1997), doesn't include as much historical information as I'd like, its color photographs are a true feast for the collector.

Objects of Desire, by Thurman Freund (Penguin, 1995). If you have no interest in antiques, this book will make you a believer. If you love the antique world, it will increase your enthusiasm. This tale of the history, re-discovery, and eventual fate of a number of pieces is as gripping and suspenseful as any best-selling thriller.

Walkingsticks, by Ulrich Klever (Schiffer Publishing, 1996; originally Verlag Georg D. W. Callwey, Munich, 1984). A prize, this one. Rich in information and wonderful photographs. *Walkingsticks* will provide a solid ground of information about the cane as weapon, musical instrument, automaton, and smoking accoutrement. Includes a value guide.

Note: The late W. Stewart Woodfill, former owner of the Grand Hotel, amassed a collection of 222 walking sticks, of which 133 are displayed at the hotel in a custom-designed English mahogany cabinet. Woodfill bristled when people referred to them as canes, stating, "Canes are for invalids."

A favorite publication of mine, the monthly *Maine Antique Digest. M.A.D.* (published by Samuel Pennington), offers articles about the industry, photos of antiques, prices that will give you a general idea of the market, and an extensive calendar of shows and auctions.

The cookbook I picked up at the fort is ti-tled *History from the Hearth: A Colonial Michilimackinac Cookbook*, by Sally Eustice (Mackinac State Historic Parks, 1997). Sheila's thrilled with this impressive publication and plans to try out some of the eighteenth-century recipes soon. (I've requested that she skip the muskrat stew.)

As you've now learned, I have a passion for cuff links. One of my favorite books is *Cuff Links*, by Susan Jonas and Marilyn Nissenson (Harry N. Abrams, Inc., paperback edition, 1999). Although this book does not give values or specific guidelines for cuff link identification, I recommend it as a visual and historical introduction. It offers nearly 200 color plates, many of which showcase the links on shirting fabric.

Asia Graham's account of her extensive collection of black memorabilia intrigued me, so I picked up *The Art and History of Black Memorabilia*, by Larry Vincent Buster (Clarkson N. Potter, Inc., 2000). This impressive-looking work comes highly recommended by Whoopi Goldberg, Ossie Davis, and various experts in the field.

Blanche says that *Victoria: The Charms of Tea* (Hearst Books, 1991) not only includes mouthwatering recipes but also shares excerpts from novels on the custom of tea. *The Pleasures of Afternoon Tea*, by Angela Hynes (HP Books, 1987), shares a well-grounded history as well as suggestions for establishing the taking of tea and many recipes.

It turns out Cal Brookner is a barbecue connoisseur. His favorite book is the *Jack Daniel's Old Time Barbecue Cookbook*, by Vince Staten (Sulgrave Press, 1995). Rich with folklore, over one hundred color photos,